Pizza Porn

Pizza Porn

Sudhir Kekre

LiFi Publications Pvt. Ltd.
New Delhi

Published by:
LiFi Publications Pvt. Ltd.
211, 2nd Floor, Gagandeep
12, Rajendra Place, New Delhi – 110 008, India
Phone : (011) 2574 1000
E-mail : info@lifipublications.com
Web : www.lifipublications.com

ISBN 13: 978-93-82536-02-4 ISBN 10: 93-82536-02-7

First published in 2013

Cataloging in Publication Data—DK
[Courtesy: D.K. Agencies (P) Ltd. <docinfo@dkagencies.com>]

Kekre, Sudhir, 1961-
Pizza porn / Sudhir Kekre.
p. cm.
Novel.
ISBN 9789382536024
ISBN 9382536027
1. Indic fiction (English). I. Title.

DDC 823.92 23

Printed in India by D.K. Fine Art Press (P) Ltd., Delhi – 52

This book is dedicated to the delightful spirit and mystique of Manipal. It is the spirit of inclusion.

This oyster city teaches you to respect people for what they are and not what they pretend to be.

When the memory of this beautiful city refused to fade even after a year of leaving, this book was natural. It simply goes to prove what this city means to a Manipalite.

'You can take him out of Manipal but you can't take Manipal out of him.'

My baker's dozen – MUCHAS GRACIAS

There was a Hakim in old Hyderabad. He sold a potion to increase the male libido. It was made from herbs, crushed pearls, snake venom and some reptile skins. He claimed that it was multi times more potent than Viagra. When I asked him the veracity of his claim, he just winked.

The Hakim, in a rare burst of poetic creativity, named his potion 'Palang tod' which literally meant one which could break the cot. It did not leave any scope for ambiguity. When I applauded him for his creativity, he patted my back and told me, "When I can write, even you can." I believed him. Now it is not important how I knew him. He was my prime motivator. Without trying palang tod, my creative juices started flowing. So my first acknowledgement. Thank you Hakimji. As a tribute, you find honourable mention in my next novel.

Writing can be very lonely. One should be lucky to have the support of a loving family. I thank my stars I had one. In this modern world, people talk about space. My family believed in giving total space. Living under the same roof, we only met on facebook and talked through chat and LOLed when we found something funny. Thank you folks for never letting me feel lonely.

Onal Bhandare. You were my back bone. You kept editing my novel right up to the day of your wedding. Thank you. If we still find mistakes, we can blame the Bhandares for it.

Anil Kekre, my dear elder brother. Thanks for providing the endless supply of my whisky. Whisky truly is for creativity what ink is for pen.

Piroj Kekre. Thank you sister for making me fat with your delicious food. I couldn't move out of my chair which made it possible to complete the novel in time.

Smita Kekre, my Bhabhi, thanks for the continuous procession of tea.

Yugesh Kekre, my nephew. Thanks for your weird sense of humour. If I had inculcated all that you suggested, I would have been writing this either from the Jail or from the Himalayas.

Sundeep Agarwal. Thanks for believing that I could write. It needed a certain amount of bravery. You not only gave lip service but put in many thankless hours of hard work in proof reading and formatting.

Power Aids and Nagender Sharma. Thanks for allowing me the space in your office. Sadly what I may miss is not your office but your large supply of Chivas Regals and Hundred Pipers.

Kailash Chandra Sharma. Thanks for your confidence that I could never complete my novel and for doubting my sincerity. It was like a kick on the back side which forced me on.

NVR Pradeep and NVR Sandeep. Those fabulous twins who were my apartment mates as well. Thanks boys for giving me an insight into the student life in Manipal. Without your support, this book wouldn't have materialized.

Tanmay Sharma. You cheeky little monkey. Every time you asked me with a twinkle if I was writing Pizza Porn, I winced. To avoid hearing it from a ten-year old, I fast tracked. So thank you.

Ms. Gitanjali Chaterjee. Thanks for taking the pains to correct my manuscript. I am sure there were a million mistakes. But your keen eyes missed nothing.

Mr. Rakesh Sharma. Sir, this has been possible only due to your dedication and sincerity. Without your steadfast support, this would have been another archived document on my laptop.

Mr. Ramesh Mittal. Sir, you are a boon to the business of publishing. You are a true professional and a humble person. I look forward to a long association.

Finally to all the dear readers. Thank you for buying my book (which I assume you did!)

Now Invest your money wisely. Save it for my next one.

I

Pizza is so much like sex.
When it is good, it is very good.
When it is bad, it is still pretty good.
(Anonymous)

'Why Pizza? Are you crazy?' We were in a steamy massage parlor in one of the side alleys of Bangkok. The room was large and partially dark with nothing but a row of cubicles separated by nylon nets, each cubicle just enough to accommodate a sweaty naked body on a simple but clean mattress. It was not a place where one could discuss business plans. But for someone who ate croissants with hot and spicy sambhar, it wasn't strange. When you lived with Nachiket long enough, the word 'surprise' lost its aura. Nothing he did was ordinary.

These cubicles afforded little privacy but no one really cared. Flesh in Thailand was just a commodity and inhibition an unnecessary baggage. Whatever privacy existed there was unintentional because the adjacent building was so close by that it obstructed the free passage of light. I could see the contours of the girl in the next cubicle. Thankfully Nachiket was not visible. All I could hear was his voice.

'You think Sonia Gandhi is the best known import from Italy? Wrong. She is not even second best. The answer is pasta.' He was quiet for a moment. I think the girl had tapped him to turn over. That gave him time to do his statistics. 'At best you could say she is the third best.' Luckily there was no one from the Congress Party there, or else he would have been grilled alive like a tandoori chicken.

Suddenly he let out a groan. We had to relinquish politics and business for another time, as we now got into the shower for the final cleansing ritual. When it comes to personal hygiene, the Thais are unmatched. I have more showers in a day here than what I have in a week back home.

We felt light as feather and found ourselves gliding back to the hotel forgetting all about pizzas, business or Italy. This was Bangkok, a hedonist's delight! Business could wait.

✦

'Men are such creeps!' Jelena, my neighbour and a self-confessed lesbian would condescendingly comment. 'They are worse than Leslie.' Leslie was her German shepherd bitch. 'Leslie comes in heat only twice a year. But these pigs are perpetually in heat.' She had a point. Sex isn't a biological need for humans. It is an obsession. Nachiket walked into our life just to prove her right.

I had first met Nachiket in Miami by chance. He had come on a business trip and needed a place to stay for six months. I was looking for a roommate who was a perfect stranger. I believe in the maxim that an unknown devil is better than a known one. His maxim was any devil who could give him a shelter was better than a devil who couldn't.

Nachiket suffered me because he had no other option. A, he didn't have a car and B, because one has to eat to survive. There was no public transport in Miami and he was a pure vegetarian. In Miami, it was easier to find Shakira and sleep with her rather than finding a vegetarian restaurant. Till I met him, I didn't know this. I knew no one who was a total vegetarian. I come from a Brahmin family and like all nice Brahmin boys; I became a devout meat eater once I touched the shores of America. Now the only vegetables that I ate were the tomatoes, lettuce and onion in the burger. It was not that I did not love animals. But I loved myself more than them. Someone has to die so that someone else could live.

One day Nachiket suddenly asked me if they gave discounts in Club Pink Pussycat if one took a monthly membership. He made me realize then that even vegetarians can be fun. After that he became my closest friend.

Pink Pussycat was what Americans so charmingly call a 'Gentlemen's club' and what we Indians so derisively call a strip joint. It was located on the northeastern part of the Miami International Airport. Pink Pussycat and Tootsie's were to Indians what Taj Mahal was to an American tourist visiting India.

What impressed me was not that he could imagine such a brilliant idea. It had to come one day. One didn't have to be Einstein to realize that. He was on a business visa and was spending his rupees in dollars which meant that for every forty rupees he spent, he got just one dollar's worth and he wasn't making many rupees either.

He earned my respect because of the timing of his thought. He could think about girls even when he was starving and we were foraging for food. But soon I realized that his personality had more folds than a *laccha* paratha, that delectable Indian bread, and as these facets unraveled, my respect for him grew. I gave him my ultimate seal of approval when I realized that like me, he traveled light. There was no extra baggage of morality.

His tryst with vegetarianism gave him a cult following. There is nothing that the Americans love more than someone a bit off their orbit – This guy was a total alien.

Ask any American to name a vegetarian food and ninety percent of them would say chicken. Ask an Indian to name a non vegetarian food and almost hundred percent would say chicken. The Americans thought that only herbivorous animals ate greens and the cows were meant to be eaten. The Indians treated cows as God. For the Americans Nachu was a freak. That they did not call him so obviously showed that the Americans have good manners, no matter what the world says. He soon became very popular. Some of his popularity rubbed off on me too.

Till he arrived, I was practically unknown in my office. Not many even knew my name. I was referred as that 'Nerd from the far off land' but now strangers came looking for me even from other departments. I was being invited to weekend parties; girls suddenly found my accent cute. Now I knew more girls and had more invitations than the pages in my diary.

It had all begun that lazy Sunday morning when we were going to that temple of modern America, Wal-Mart, to buy our customary weekly groceries. Wal-Mart was the new church. If it was a Sunday, you had to visit Wal-Mart.

I suggested that we stop by at McDonald's on the NW 41 St. for breakfast. Donna, the girl at the counter smiled at us. We were old friends. I ordered a double quarter pounder with cheese. She had no problem with my order but when Nachiket asked for a vegetarian sandwich, she just blinked. 'No chicken, no meat. Just vegetables.' I said helpfully. She was Spanish and like most Spanish girls had more oomph than English in her. I suddenly remembered to add 'Please'. I was much like her minus the oomph.

The girl smiled brightly and soon Miss Sunshine came back with a plateful of lettuce and tomatoes. 'No meat, no chicken. Just vegetables,' she smiled cheerfully. Nachiket smiled equally brightly and thanked her for her kindness. The only audible words that came out of him after looking at the foliage were, 'I feel like a goat.'

The jokes continued. The second time it happened was when I took him to Saw Grass Mill, Florida's largest shopping mall. He enjoyed shopping and couldn't stop talking. Not until we sat down for lunch.

The waiter in that posh restaurant was a sharp young math student earning his school fees by waiting at tables. We repeated our request mechanically. 'No chicken and no meat please.' He emerged from the kitchen with deep furrows on his forehead.

'Well sir, there is nothing like a "pure vegetarian dish". But we can't let you go hungry. So I have an idea' – said the Math Major helpfully. 'I will bring the whole dish and you can pick out the vegetables and perhaps your friend here could eat the rest.' He beamed at us obviously unaware that in India the rules of vegetarianism are very strict. Forget about picking vegetables from a meat dish, many vegetarians don't even eat at the same table where there is any meat.

My petrified friend matched the waiter's somber expression and thought for a while and then ordered plain rice which he said he could eat with yoghurt. 'Safest food. I bet you can't adulterate it with meat,' he grinned wickedly, happy at his own cleverness. Sadly he had underestimated the carnivorous habits of the Americans. The so-called 'plain rice' had been boiled in pork broth. Nachu had no option how he would have to forego lunch. I was left with the only honourable thing to do. I had to eat alone.

When the steaming delicious meal arrived, Nachiket's defenses crumbled. He was starving. He remembered the Lindt chocolates we had bought. He asked the waiter if it was alright to have his chocolate bar. The conscientious waiter was as fascinated with the new principles of 'vegetarianism' as he would be to learn the complexities of Euler's theorem or Descartes rules of signs. He took the half eaten chocolate bar from his hand and read out the ingredients. Nachu was soon left clutching his throat. It had lard in it!

✦

No one epitomized the true American better than Nachiket's manager Duncan. He was a man of gigantic proportion but had the heart of an angel. There is no noble and greater reason to visit a pub than treating a foreign guest. Duncan invited Nachu to Chilis for a drink. He knew about his vegetarian habits and like all Americans he respected all religions. When his steak and Portobello arrived, he graciously kept picking the bell pepper and mushroom from it and offering it to Nachu, assuring him that it was cent per cent vegetarian. No meat in it he assured, wiping his fork every time.

Since then, Nachiket was scared to even touch fruit salad. 'Who knows, there might be beef chunks in it!' he would comment condescendingly. He resigned himself to a life of milk and fresh fruits.

But the God of vegetarianism smiled at him one day. It was in the Flannigan's, a cozy seafood bar and grill on the South Dixie Highway. The bartender, God's chosen messenger, suggested baked potato with sour cream.

Perfect! Nachiket hogged five of them, barely touching his Corona Beer. The genial bartender joked that in America we do it the other way round. Nachiket, licking the sour cream and grinning like a Cheshire cat, said that he was more hungry than thirsty.

Alas, his happiness was short-lived. While waiting for a connecting flight at Houston Airport, he asked me to get him some baked potato. I warned him that this was a different state, they may have different standards. But we didn't have much choice.

Now, the Idahoans are a hardworking and proud lot and love to show off their large farm produce.

The chef who was from Idaho, picked up a huge Idaho potato, large enough to feed an entire family, scooped it expertly and generously filled it with a large helping of shredded beef. Alas, the potato had to go into the trash bin!.

In a month's time, Nachiket realized that ordering French fries was the safest bet.

I felt sorry for him.

'Try potato wedges for a change,' I suggested.

He almost fainted when the wedges were served with delicate slices of fried bacon!!!

His six months flew by fast and then it was almost time to return to India, I can bet on it that, no living Indian had been given such a rousing farewell. His legions of fans were sad to see him leave and kept in touch even after he left. They enquired if he was happy back home and whether he was eating well. This many times bitten and never shy guy wanted to be sure in India as well. When he enquired in a typical south Indian restaurant what did they cook the plain rice in, the waiter looked at him strangely. 'Water! And that's why it's known as plain rice. But if you like meat, we also serve mutton and chicken biryani!'

In India we have a national animal and a national flower. But we don't have a national fruit. If we did, it had to be the orange. We Indians are like oranges. From the outside we look like one. Remove the skin and we fall apart. There is perhaps no country which is more communal and casteist than ours. In India we are divided into various castes. That is something which was traditionally inherited by us and for which we ourselves can only be partially blamed. But we even create divisions where there are none.

We have carried our separatist agenda even across the seven seas. In the US, the Brahmins, who are traditionally the upper caste, are the Indians who have citizenship. The next in the pecking order are the green card holders or the permanent citizens. The business visa holders are the untouchables.

But apart from these, there is also another broad division. The second generation Indians are derisively called ABCD – American born confused desis. These are the mutants who are neither fully Indian nor fully American. Not to be outdone, the ABCD call the new arrivals FOBs – Fresh off boats. The ABCD consider themselves and find it below their dignity to hobnob with the FOBs. The FOBs are the poor cousins. The bumbling villagers. The FOBs on their part do nothing to endear themselves to the ABCDs. They stick to their own clan and make no attempts to mingle with the ABCDs.

I was one of the FOBs but I made no attempt to join any camp. It was more a geographical compulsion than any great principled stand. There were not many Indians in Miami. Searching for another Indian was again, to use my own cliché, like finding Shakira. So when we felt homesick, we either went to India or to New Jersey. There was a joke in the desi circles about NJ. When you are flying, you would know that you have reached NJ from the saris hanging outside to dry. In India, people do not use washing machines and dry their clothes in the sun by hanging them on a string. The sari was therefore a silly metaphor.

But New Jersey is a veritable little India. There are more Gujaratis there than there are in the whole of Gujarat. The Gujaratis came to the USA bringing all their quirks and idiosyncrasies. It is not uncommon to meet a Patel, who in-between taking a deep drag from his snuff box would enquire, *'Hmm, kya Tejas bhai, majama che?'* (Are you fine, Tejas?)

What made NJ feel like home was that the large Indian population brought with them all their disorderliness and rule breaking habits. The Americans would be exasperated.

Suddenly someone would be seen running across the road. I once heard an exasperated American after screeching to a halt, remark at one such Indian, 'Hey, you don't have to run anymore. You have reached America.'

The FOBs in New Jersey have a very set routine and this routine is set in stone. Nothing can alter the routine, specially on weekends. If he is a true blooded FOB, he will get up at 12 in the afternoon and then reach the Mughal for a buffet lunch. The buffet would be a lavish spread from all over India right from the 'tangy chaat' to the succulent tandoori chicken to the crispy masala dosa. A true blue blooded Indian wouldn't be seen drinking anything except mango lassi.

After a sumptuous lunch, it would be shopping time; a time to visit Costco or Wal-Mart and hunt for bargain sales. The important thing to bear in mind is the bargain, no matter if it is required or not. If there is a bargain, it is meant to be purchased. It can always be used in future. It is not uncommon to see Indians dragging shopping carts loaded with a year's supply of toilet papers.

While returning, they check for the latest Hindi movie release. Check would be the wrong word to use since it didn't matter which movie it was, it had to be watched. After the movie, the night ended in Chutney Mary for another round of buffet.

This whole description of NJ has a very deep emotional connection. This is where Nachu and I really bonded.

We were visiting some friends in New Jersey. Nachiket was a movie buff. We went to watch a movie after the mandatory lunch at the Mughal. Bollywood had a timeworn yet successful theme of two brothers lost in the village fair when they were kids only to be re-united when they are strapping handsome youths, each recognizing the other because of a tattoo or a ring or a chain around the neck with a family picture in the locket. This movie was no different.

I was totally untouched but not Nachiket. He was very quiet. The corny movies influenced him in many ways. I asked him several times what was the matter but he kept silent. Then suddenly he blurted out, 'We are long last brothers.' But how could he be so sure, I joked. We did not have any family tattoo on our asses to come to the conclusion.

'We both love porn.' He simply said. Now that was a clincher that I couldn't dispute.

He indeed was my brother, never mind who our mother was. Our friendship, strong otherwise, was now cemented.

✦

Thailand was the perfect retreat for people like me and Nachiket. From the minimalists to the epicurean, from the ascetics to the hedonists, from the body to the soul, there was something for everyone. It was an exciting and heady concoction of delightful contradictions. A land ravaged by nature and humans alike and constantly under turmoil. The Thais camouflage their sorrows in a dazzling show of happiness. I was still exploring and with my keen eye could have observed more. But the brazen physical had more attraction for me than the metaphysical.

There could be various ways of exploring Krung Thep or the City of Angels; Bangkok, to the ordinary. There were the nerds who came armed with travel guides or the pink panthers who relied on Dreaded Ned. I had a far simpler solution. Laziness made me creative. Find the best cab. If there was something to be seen, the cab driver would certainly know of it.

I was lucky. I was looking for a guide, I found God.

The God was called Tonsuk. Aptly, we began our journey from a monastery. It had nothing to do with religion. At least from my end.

'If we visit the Gem Gallery, you don't have to pay anything to me. The Gem Gallery pays our gas bill for bringing customers. You don't have to buy anything either.' I was impatient but not stupid. 'In Rome do as Indians do.' Every rupee saved was a rupee earned. It wouldn't matter if we gawked at stones we would never afford or care to buy as long as we were saving money.

The Gem Gallery was dazzling.

Even to someone as prosaic as me, it was remarkable There were expensive rubies and sapphires and diamonds, all transformed into *object d'art*. The jewellery dazzled me but failed to impress me. I was looking for jewels of another kind.

On the way to the Gem Gallery, we had stopped by at a monastery. Tonsuk was a religious man. But I saw it as an unnecessary pit stop. Yet I had to humor him if I had to see any of the fabled night life of Bangkok.

The monastery was a very peaceful place. But it held no interest for me. Tonsuk tried to involve me in their elaborate rituals. But I was in a hurry. One monk smiled benignly and gently rebuked me, 'Lord Buddha is everywhere and blesses every one, more so the people who need him more.' I looked at him to see if he was being sarcastic. But his face was deadpan.

Tonsuk was a treasure trove of knowledge of the night life of Bangkok. He showed us everything. It bordered from the elegant to the weird, from the erotic to outright repulsive. We sat through rapturously in the Mambo show and saw the breathtakingly beautiful she boys dance with nimble feet and delicate expressions to the tune of Bollywood hits. Nachu swore that one of them danced better and looked prettier than Aishwarya Rai. We visited the Go-Go bars, the massage parlors, cheap bars and trendy discos. We went to weird shows, too revolting to even write about. But soon we got bored and we thought he had run out of tricks and it was time to say goodbye to him. But I hadn't called him God for nothing.

As we were having breakfast, Tonsuk arrived with a big grin.

'Tonight, no shows, no bars. I take you to meet a vely special friend. All youls.' It was our little joke playing on his pronunciation. Even though it was lame, he always politely laughed.

Nachu had enough of Tonsuk. He simply kept dunking his croissants in his tom yum soup nonchalantly.

✦

There are some areas where we Indians are invincible. The Americans can conquer the moon or Iraq, but they can never dream of conquering the Indian traffic or reaching an address in India unaided. No Google Map or GPS has been built for that. When you look at the traffic in India, you realize what a true democracy is. The dogs, cows and buffaloes have equal rights on the road as do human beings. While applying for a driver's license in the US, there is a question about yielding space at traffic signals. In India, no self-respecting human being or dog or buffalo yields space to anyone. The streets have also one more important function. These are home to many bovines and canines. When my American friends visit Delhi, they are so excited to see cows and dogs on the streets. Daphne, an American friend once, was delighted while on a visit to India, and said 'I want to see elephants' as if I was the director of a zoo. 'Yeah, sure. Watch out, we use them to cross the busy streets,' I said cheekily. But the sarcasm was lost on the poor girl whose knowledge about India was the stereotypical American one that it was the land of snake charmers and naked fakirs, software engineers and call centers.

Now even hypothetically if they negotiated the traffic, they would still find it difficult to reach the address. The same girl Daphne took two hours to reach 'Trishna', an upscale restaurant in Kala Ghoda in Mumbai from Leopald Café in Colaba Causeway which was just a ten minutes walk. She had committed a cardinal sin. She had referred to a travel book with maps and the compass from her iPhone. No Indian would dream of doing that. We are not dumb. But still we have a sign language of hands which is more effective than any incomprehensible map or any esoteric compass. It has worked for ages and we see no reason to change our habits.

I, therefore, always smugly thought that I could negotiate any roads in the world and find any address anywhere from Ghatkopar to Timbuktu.

But Bangkok punctured my ego. We drove through an intricate maze of lanes and by-lanes till I totally lost track. The only way I could reach the hotel back, if I were lost, was to hire a cab.

I looked back from the back street. The city lights were running away from us fast. The roads were now dusty and bumpy leaving a trail of dust behind us. I looked out through the window. The whole place had a much neglected look. There were vast expanses of barren land. We had reached the outskirts of the city.

We could now see women carrying water from a distance which meant that there was a settlement close by. I wondered where he was taking me. I could see rows and rows of shanties once again reminding me of Mumbai and its vast slums. In Mumbai next to the railway line, among mounds of trash and open sewers, these hutments house the poor immigrants coming from far off Uttar Pradesh or Tamil Nadu. These shanties looked similar. Only there were no trash mountains or open sewers.

For a moment, I was disappointed and rued my decision to come with Tonsuk. Nachu was right. This guy had clearly run out of ideas. What was he going to show me now I wondered. Poverty porn. I wasn't a westerner. I had seen poverty up close. I wondered what was Nachu doing? It was only later I learnt that he was eavesdropping on a rich Italian in a spa.

But there was nothing I could do now. The apology for a road ended abruptly. Tonsuk got down from the cab signaling us to follow him.

We walked through narrow alleys, careful not to bang our heads against the bamboos jutting out from the framework of the huts. I couldn't see even my sandals in the darkness, but was sure that by now they were coated with a layer of dust. I braced myself for a long and uncomfortable walk. Just when I thought the ordeal would never end, he stopped and led me into a shanty. I had now resigned myself to an evening of boredom. Probably Tonsuk had decided that we needed a lesson in minimalism before we left.

We lowered our heads and walked inside through the low door. It was just another shanty. There was not much furniture but whatever was there, was neatly placed. Tonsuk introduced me to an old man with a toothy smile. We were made to sit on small stools. A woman appeared from inside with a can of Singha beer which I gratefully accepted. The long drive and the walk had made me thirsty. I finished it in a gulp. Instantly I was offered another. I was embarrassed. I did not know how to say no. It would be unfair to accept hospitality for free. But the Thais are very sensitive people. They get offended very quickly. Tonsuk had to handle this. I accepted the beer anyway.

Tonsuk spoke to him in a hushed tone. I could barely hear or understand anything. Whenever they looked at me, I nodded my head vigorously and smiled weakly. They smiled back. This works in most of Asia. The Americans used to joke about how the Indians bobbed their heads the same way for yes and no. Nachiket had explained nonchalantly, 'It is a culture thing.' I had looked at him strangely. 'What has culture got to do with it?'

'You have a better answer?' I shook my head, this time meaning no.

'Then shut up.'

This discussion seemed over and Tonsuk turned to me. The deal was clinched he whispered in my ears but the money had to be paid up front. 'For what?', I asked. Tonsuk gave his widest grin. When he did that you simply paid. Suddenly Mr. Toothy Smile bent forward and showed two fingers. I looked at Tonsuk. He nodded. Two meant 200 baht. 'For the beer,' he explained, smiling toothily. I could have had it for 25 baht outside. But I knew the theory of supply and demand. I gave him 300 baht and asked him to get me one more beer. I didn't know for what I had paid the remaining money.

Just then, my investment walked in coyly. I almost spilled my beer. She was stunning; Tonsuk was really the God of all good things! The girl smiled and bowed her head and folded her hands in Wai, the Thai way of welcome. I stood up to repeat the Wai. 'Wai' was similar to our '*Namaste*' but much more aesthetic. Tonsuk, the toothy man and the other woman giggled, the girl blushed and I just stared. She had cast a spell on me. The old man again whispered and Tonsuk translated 'If you go to your hotel, they will charge you 1000 baht for bringing a guest. In addition you will have to pay for the return cab. There's a hotel here which charges by the hour, 400 baht for an hour.' This guy surely knew how to do business. The beers didn't seem expensive anymore. He robbed Peter to pay whatever his name was. But I wasn't complaining.

Tonsuk, the girl and I bid goodbye to the couple, folding our hands and bowing our head, and then started for the hotel. The hotel looked like some of the cheap motels in New Jersey. It wasn't ostentatious but looked comfortable. Tonsuk, drove his cab into the backyard and stopped in front of what looked like a garage. Suddenly a man appeared from nowhere. Tonsuk spoke to him in Thai. The man nodded and asked us to follow him. I expected him to take us to the front lobby. But instead he took us to the garage. There behind the cars, concealed from outside, were rows of rooms. I was scared and asked Tonsuk if it was safe. He smiled in his reassuring manner. Most hotels in Bangkok made extra money this way, he said. We had to pay the money in advance and in cash and no receipt was given.

The room was large and clean but unpretentiously furnished with one giant round bed in the center leaving visitors in no doubt about the use of the room. It had one cheap TV, some fresh towels and a box of condoms on the table, which I first thought was soap. The girl giggled when I told her so. She had a beautiful smile. She pointed to the bathroom. There was liquid soap inside. Again I was struck by the cleanliness. The white Turkish towels were extraordinarily white which delighted me since I have a fetish for cleanliness.

I paid Tonsuk and told him I would find my way back. He wouldn't budge, concerned about my safety, that good man. I smiled and told him I was a big boy and could take care of myself. Only after giving me his mobile number, his card, and extracting a promise that I would call him if there was an emergency, he left.

As soon as he left, the girl ordered some beer and led me to the shower. I sighed. God, not another shower! My skin would peel away one day from all the showers, I thought.

Later she switched off most of the lights but kept the TV on.

I was intrigued when she turned up the TV volume. Then she went inside and turned the faucet over the tub at full! The TV and the shower made a deafening racket. My nerves jangled. But I kept quiet. 'Culture thing' I thought. Thank you Nachiket.

She came to the bed shyly and sat down in one corner. I was caught in a dilemma. She looked so innocent that I didn't want to touch her. But the raging hormones inside me wouldn't let me be quiet. I decided to be gentle. I kissed her lightly. Her mouth was soft and sweet. She lowered her eyes. Tenderly, I held her breast as I kissed her again. They were small but firm. She was painfully shy but I was in no hurry. I took my time undressing her. Her skin was soft and gossamer like the petals of a rose. She had narrow hips and a slender waist. Her shyness heightened my desire. Was I the first one in her life? I felt an added responsibility.

Each day in Thailand had been a learning experience. My lesson that night, with a shock, was that appearances could be highly deceptive. She was shy only till the lights went off. And then she started moaning even before I had settled down to business. Initially I felt proud of my expertise. I had touched her at the right spots I thought. But then gradually the volume of her moans increased. I may be vain but I know my limitations. She was clearly faking it. She started screaming like we were acting in a blue film. Now I understood why the TV was on in full volume. I felt cheated. But suddenly I was ambushed.

I couldn't believe my eyes or ears. The meek lamb that had entered was now a roaring tigress. I was blown away like a dry leaf in a hurricane, carrying my romantic and tender feelings along with it.

This was no love making. It was raw sex. I felt like as if I was drowning in an ocean and gasping for breath. We hit the crescendo and climaxed together with a war cry from her. It was incredible. I couldn't have ever imagined that she was such a pro. I must concede it was much better than the romance I was planning.

It was later that Tonsuk enlightened me. The Thais believed that moaning turns the western men on. Me and western! Was she blind? No she wasn't, but she could recognize an American driving license, he said. She wasn't naive.

I felt utterly exhausted. It felt like a tsunami had just passed over me.

She asked with genuine concern, 'Jay happy? I make him happy?' I had to assure her a hundred times. 'Jay happy. Velly velly happy!' When she asked me again, I couldn't take it any more. To prove I was happy I took out my wallet and pulled out a wad of notes and gave it to her. She folded her hands and bowed. The Thais could steal your pant with that sweet smile and 'wai'.

As I was pulling up my pant, I was still numb with the experience. Before leaving, I routinely checked my wallet and then froze. It was empty. In my anxiety to comfort her, I had accidentally pulled out the entire wad of notes and given it to her. The sorceress now had all my money! There was no way I could reach my hotel. Dear Tonsuk had made me leave behind all my credit cards. (Never take cards, he had said) and the cash which I was carrying was in her dainty hands. I was standing there penniless!

She was wise and her beautiful eyes had seen everything. She had seen that in my enthusiasm I had pulled the entire wad of notes and I didn't have any money left to go back to my hotel.

She suddenly opened here palm and spread it in front of me. It had all the money that I had given her. I was dumbstruck!

'Jay take. It is jay money'. My eyes were wide. I was a man of the world. I had seen life and had been mugged, robbed and stripped in three continents. But here was a hooker who had my last penny and yet! I was overcome with her generosity. This could happen only in Thailand! Was it the Singha that I was drinking copiously or the memory of that incredible sex we just had or was it her act of utter selflessness, I suddenly took her in my arms and proposed, 'Suwanee, will you marry me?'

I was cursing myself as I waited for her to say yes and thinking of the horror that would await me when I returned home. But she suddenly held my face in her hands and with tears said 'Jay good. Velly good.' then what followed was a torrent of words of unmistakable regret. She was refusing my offer. I wanted to cry out in relief. It was like I had two orgasms that night! I had escaped narrowly. This night was turning weirder and weirder and I had to leave immediately before I committed another faux pas. But I was in a dilemma.

I had to reach my hotel. I needed money. So I took 50 baht from her, the exact amount it would take in the sky train to transport me from this fairy to ground zero! I felt cheap. But walking was an option. But feeling cheap was a better one. It wouldn't be the first time in my life anyway.

I asked her gratefully if I could see her again the next day. Tearfully she said, she wanted tonight to be the best night of her life (or so I believed! My imagination goes wild when I think of someone praising me.) I thanked her profusely. I had forgotten in my emotional turmoil what she had done to me. Two days of such raw passion and I would be dead meat. She had unwittingly bailed me out once again. With a heavy heart and a hearty *wai*, we bid good bye to each other.

It was only when I was standing in the sky train that the absurdity of the whole thing suddenly struck me and I began to laugh uncontrollably. Thankfully there were not many people around. No one even bothered to glance at me. Most of them were tourists. There were also tired Thais returning after may be another hard night. They had an expression of indifference which could mean anything from I don't care to I know you are crazy. Only an Australian with a Thai girl smiled at me and said, 'I know it's this country. It can make you crazy'. I shook my head and said, 'Nah, it's not them. It's me'. 'Whatever' the bloke shrugged.

I was still laughing even when I got off the train. I had been rejected by many girls. Most thought I wasn't husband material. But tonight I had hit the bottom of the barrel. Even a prostitute had rejected me!

I could feel the crack of dawn though I couldn't see it. The sky scrapers hid everything. I was now crossing the bridge leading to my hotel. There was the familiar beggar woman with her child, sitting on the bridge. She smiled as she recognized me. I used to drop some coins in her pail whenever I walked past her. I smiled back and dug into my pocket's to realize I had no money. I pulled out both pockets to show her my empty pockets. She grinned.

I looked at the woman again. Probably I paid more money for my hotel per day then what she made in a fortnight. Yet this morning she had at least some coins in her pail. I had none. I was perhaps the poorest guy in Thailand at that moment.

Then epiphany struck. I was nothing without money.

As I walked into the rising sun, a new dawn was rising inside me. I realized the worth of money. Suddenly I recalled my conversation with Nachiket that night in the parlour. Business. We had to start a business. Buddhism taught renunciation. But in this land of yellow flowing robes known for its austerity, I rediscovered my hunger for making money. The monk was right. Lord Buddha had guided me in his own mysterious way. He had his epiphany under a tree. But I had mine on a bridge.

✦

A week is a long long time. Last week when we had landed in Thailand and started enjoying our holidays, I had almost apologized to myself for all the time wasted in the office. The dreary hours spent in an office could have been more productive. We were out of work and enjoying it and now in a week's time I discovered the necessity of having a job. If you want to have fun, you need money. For earning money, you had to work. It was no rocket science. What had taken me so long to understand it?

Good news and bad news are like the Indian couple. They never divorce each other and always come in pairs.

And so one morning we received the two news together. Bad news, that the American gaming company we worked for had terminated our contract. We would no longer be outsourcing for them. The good news, they had settled all our accounts till date and transferred the balance money into our account leaving us rich.

Uncle Sam had kicked us between our balls but he had done it in style. He did not leave us starving. There was no option but to close shop. I had visited Sunnyvale twice to convince and also find new business. I had failed. California may be in the USA but most of the business there is either owned by the Chinese or Indians. Asians are a very tight fisted lot. You hit someone in the funny bone, he would wince with pain and open his fist. Try hitting an Asian. He would wince with pain but the fist would still remain closed.

The Koreans we were working for were outsourcing now to Kazakhstan who charged peanuts on an hourly basis, much lesser than even the salary we paid to our employees. Damn these small countries! They were killing our business and our government was a mute spectator. Couldn't the government sign some kind of a trade agreement with them? Or shouldn't they approach the United Nations? Nachiket suggested that we were proud people and wouldn't go and beg to our government or allow our government to beg to the United Nations. So the most respectable thing to do would be to clear our employees' accounts and close shop.

We were good paymasters. We paid them three months salary even though there was a notice period of only one month, wished them luck and bid our goodbyes. The surprised girls looked like a deer caught in a headlight on the highway at night. They didn't know how to react. Caught between happiness and sadness, they didn't know whether to laugh or to cry. They were losing a job which was not permanent, yet it brought food on their table every month. But they were happy because now they had three months to look for a new job. We left them with their mouths open and undecided whether to laugh or cry.

We were now left with an empty office and some money in the bank. We had to decide what to do next.

It is a paradox that we take eons to decide unimportant stuff like what to wear for a dinner party but the important decisions in life are taken in a jiffy. The trouble with money is that it is never too much but we always looked at the brighter side of life. It was enough for us to buy us a luxurious vacation in Thailand. It took us lesser time to pack our stuff than it took to decide and before we could even utter 'done', we found ourselves on board a flight to Bangkok.

✦

I was sure that the Money Exchange counter would open before I could find Nachiket. Expecting him to return to the hotel before noon would be too much. I sat on the staircase of the exchange booth and waited for it to open, dreaming about a beer and a sandwich, the prostitute and my life in general. I was hungry and the sandwich took precedence.

✦

A few months ago, I had been a professional. When and how the proverbial entrepreneurial bug bit me, I do not know. Honestly, it was a Hobson's choice. I was tired of slaving for others. So there was no other option. Besides, it is not a very happy feeling to realize that you are not even thirty, jobless, penniless and living in India with some nosey Parker neighbor. My neighbor was a gossipy lady Mrs. Sehgal who lived with her docile husband and smoking hot twins. She was an obnoxious woman who interfered more in my life than in her own children's. It bothered her more than my parents that I had no work and spared no opportunity to make me realize what a good-for-nothing I was.

She would come to our house without even knocking and sit for hours pontificating on why I should find a job and get married. It was like a stuck record.

She would invariably begin with the sentence 'Our ancestors were wise people and for everything they have planned there is a reason. There are four stages in a Hindu's life. Now you are an adult and so you must enter the *Grihastha Ashram*, marry and have children. Otherwise how would your family name continue?' or 'You should be ashamed of yourself. You are not young anymore and still your father has to work.

You must earn and help your parents. Who will look after them, if not you?' In a way, she can stake her claim for making an enterpreneur out of me.

One afternoon, I was bored with nothing to do. I picked up an old copy of *Playboy* just to kill time. Just when I became horny and started playing with myself, she entered without knocking. She was scandalized. 'No wonder there are dark circles under your eyes. All that semen being wasted!'. She had to help me, she said with a stern face. I could have told her a hundred ways she could have helped but sulked instead.

She went to a swamiji who assured her that all my problems in life were because I masturbated and that he could cure me of that disease if I was brought to his ashram.

One day a friend who was working in the US was chatting with me. He wanted to outsource some business, would I be interested he asked? It was for an animation company in Sunnyvale. I jumped at the offer. Here was a chance to protect my honour and save me from endless discussions about my battle with a disease called onanism, its debilitating effect on my sexuality, health and general well being from entering the common neighborhood domain.

The outsourcing business had split the country vertically. There were those who hit the gravy train and those who didn't. We were heckled by the people who were left out that we were nothing but glorified laborers. I never disagreed. It didn't offer us dignity. But it brought in the dollars. I was not complaining. I was making money doing nothing. But Mrs. Sehgal was not satisfied. I had not yet visited the swamiji. Hence I was pimping to the decadent West. I thought ignoring her would be best. How little I knew about her!

One day the swamiji himself turned up at our office to 'cure' me. I was annoyed but couldn't do anything. Mother and Mrs. Sehgal were with him. He wore a saffron robe and was carrying a *jhola* (loose bag). I saw a chillum peeping out of it. Immediately I had a brainwave. I sent someone urgently to Sitaphalmandi to buy grass. The swami, unaware, asked the ladies to leave the room as he had some man to man chat to do with me. When we were alone, I whispered to him that I had some top class grass which had been smuggled from Nepal via Gorakhpur. The offer was irresistible. No blue blooded swami could refuse it.

To cut a long story short, we both ended up smoking grass together. While leaving I bribed him with some more of the stuff. He invited me to his ashram. This time as an equal.

Mrs. Sehgal never bothered me after that. She now cribbed that I was gay and incurable.

Only if she had checked it out with one of her twin daughters! I don't know which one!

Being your own boss has its own advantages. Like you could, if you wanted to, get drunk even on a hot sultry afternoon. But these advantages are like the air miles given by airlines these days. They are hardly ever used.

We didn't really work much. We had a good time spending the dollars. But now we had to bust our ass.

It was time to make a living.

✦ ✦ ✦

II

**Planning a project
is like baking a delicate apricot soufflé.
One mistake and it could fall flat.
We were lucky. Lady luck was on our side.**

Entrepreneurship is serious business. I had once attended a seminar on it and learnt that there are two types of entrepreneurs. The leaders and the followers. The leaders enter a virgin field and do pioneering work in them. For example, think of the first computers or airplanes or mobiles. The leaders make money on the novelty factor. The followers too work hard but follow one of the leaders. They refine the product and give it their brand identity. They make money because of the value addition. For instance, think of the mobiles when they were first introduced. They were heavy and cumbersome and look at them now!

We unfortunately didn't fall into either of the two categories. We were entrepreneurs by chance. Entrepreneurship demands mastery on many intricate subjects. You had to be good in finance, marketing, administration and so many things. We were good at none. We only had Lady Luck on our side. Many times I wondered, if she was a lady and on our side, why did she never sleep with us? Nachiket heard me out patiently and after a long pause commented, 'Your research has led me to conclude only one thing. You think with your dick.' I thought he was being blasé and stupid. But was he stupid alone?

We both had proprietary rights on 'stupidity'. Long after we were into pizza business, Nachu one day confessed that he suggested opening a pizzeria because he had heard a stray comment in the sauna of the Ambassador Hotel from the mouth of a wealthy Italian businessman, 'Pizza is like porn. No one can lose money in it.' We had entered a business on one stray comment!

Nachu had tossed me this idea in the massage parlor but I gave him the seal of approval the next day. So I can't absolve myself from the blame of stupidity. If he had been reckless in advising, I had not been very prudent in my approval either. My approval came in very extenuating circumstances.

We were sitting in a food court in Bangkok sipping black coffee and nursing a hangover. Nachiket, true to his weird eating habits, was eating water melon along with the coffee.

Suddenly Nachu nudged me. There in a corner sat the most gorgeous looking girl God had ever created. She was eating a pizza. Pizza had never looked so sexy. Nachiket sucked in his breath. She had not seen us but perhaps felt the heat of the intensity of our combined stares. She suddenly looked at us and smiled. Emboldened and our hangover forgotten, we walked up to her and introduced ourselves.

She smiled. 'I am O'. The Thais are smart people. They know it is difficult for foreigners to pronounce their names. So many of them just use a single letter. That is how I became Jay in Thailand. 'I love pizza. It is like sex. When it is good it is very good. When it is bad it is still pretty good,' she grinned. 'And now it is very good. Velly velly nice and juicy.' We just sat there staring. I didn't have to ask Nachiket but we could feel the taste of the soft and juicy pizza. I looked at him.

He muttered under his breath, 'Pizza-Corner.' I barely nodded. I was fantasizing. Nachiket was an amateur writer. But this time he outdid himself. Pizza and corner. Pizza-Corner. What a sexy name!

Successful businessmen write their autobiographies when they retire. I often wonder if we were successful, what we shall write.

One month later we had taken back the same office, paid the owner an extra month's rent as bribe and were now sitting with the architect and finalizing the design of Pizza-Corner. Mom wanted a puja done before we began business. I assured her that we would. Deshpande was a good man and a leading architect. He didn't accept small jobs. But he had done our uncle's large office's interiors and was returning a favor. He began with a few elementary questions that left us baffled and him flabbergasted. Why was he here? We hadn't finalized anything yet! He promised to send us a list of things to do once he reached office. The list never came. All our calls went unanswered.

We badly needed an architect. From our network we found one. He was a young man named Correa. We thought we had heard this name before. Then suddenly Nachu remembered. We had seen his designs in the book that our carpenter Ram

Bharose had brought. We somehow liked his name. It reminded us of the coral island in Pattaya. We were indeed lucky to find someone so famous. When we complimented him for that, he absentmindedly nodded his head. I thought that he was being modest. We spoke to him with a lot of deference. It was only later when our project was near completion we learnt that he wasn't Charles Correa. He was an out-of-work architect who had not even completed his degree in architecture because he thought that there was nothing more to learn from college. If we had thought for a while then, we would have known. The only chance of some celebrity being known in our circle would perhaps be Sunny Leone. But he turned out to be a blessing in disguise. This guy had no qualms about redoing his drawings. In fact, we sometimes felt guilty because if we suggested even a minor modification, he would tear up the entire drawings and redo the whole thing again.

Since we were his only client, he would spend most of his time here, sometimes even staying back for a glass of beer. We had a fridge in our office which was always stacked with beer. The beer didn't go waste. He would advise us on other issues as well.

Just like some marriages are made in heaven, there are some relations which are conceived by the lord himself. Correa and our professional relation was one of those. He was in fact brilliant. He had been selected for the IIT but felt that IIT promotes rotes. It was stifling to be among the so-called achievers whose only qualification was that they could mug up better than the others. So he had left IIT and applied at the Delhi School of Architecture. But soon he felt that he was wasting his time there as well and hence decided to take the plunge into professional life.

He really became a life member of our club when he narrated an incident from his personal life in one of our evening beer sessions. He had one day picked up a prostitute from Palika Bazaar in Delhi. This was the first underground fully air-conditioned market in India and was a notorious hot spot for escorts and pick-ups.

When he brought her to his rented *barsaati* (a small rooftop room) in Lajpat Nagar, she insisted on first getting paid. He was amused and asked her if she didn't trust him. She told him nonchalantly that it was the principle of her business. Money first.

When he was taking out the money from his pocket, she casually remarked that everyone, including he, is a prostitute. Some sell their body, others sell their souls. It hit a chord somewhere. He paid her fully but said that he wanted to only talk to her and was it fine? She said yes. He wanted to know her story.

They spent the entire evening reliving her childhood in Nepal and how she was smuggled to India via Gorakhpur at the age of thirteen and reached Lucknow where she was sold to a Madam. Sapna, that's what she said her name was, stayed there for three years and was then sold to another middleman who brought her to Delhi. They operated from an apartment in the posh South Ex. Colony. Soon she was making enough money to buy her freedom. Now that she knew all the tricks of the trade, she did not need a middleman as most of the money she earned was taken away by him by way of commission. When Correa asked her why she was still in this business, she replied that it was not easy to find a job as she was not educated. When he asked her why she didn't learn something, she said that because it was very expensive. Correa decided he would sponsor her education. She joined a beautician's course. By then Correa had decided to drop out of college and move to Hyderabad. Sapna too moved along with him to Hyderabad. She opened a beauty parlour last year and was now a successful beautician with a staff of three girls and making a decent living. She was a proud girl now. Although Correa had never asked her, she paid him a fixed amount every month. Nachu asked him if he was planning to marry her. He just smiled. Since then he was one of us. One day he brought pure grass. Such a guy automatically qualified to be the President of our club!

Ram Bharose, our Man Friday, deserves more than a passing mention. We can safely say that he was the first pillar of our company in order of arrival. Correa, Mr. Gupta and Ramchandran being the other three. He was a brilliant carpenter from a small village called Neem ka Thana in Rajasthan. We were indeed lucky to have someone like him. He was so talented that his creation for an ITC Hotel had once appeared on the cover of *Inside Outside*.

He had worked with Deshpande, the architect who had never returned our calls. I had to again use the good books of my uncle who wasn't very happy to again talk to Deshpande for us. But we promised him that this would be his last embarrassment. He just glared at us but dialed him nevertheless.

Ram Bharose, like Correa, was ear marked by Lord Ram himself for us. He had a very interesting story. When Ram Bharose was a child, a cholera epidemic had struck his village killing most of the villagers. His parents had no hope that their lone son would survive. As a last resort, they named him Ram Bharose (someone who lived on the mercy of Lord Ram), leaving his well being to Lord Rama. Miraculously Ram Bharose survived and was now there to serve us. We thanked Lord Ram for saving him. But for the Lord's benevolence, the world would have lost one of the best carpenters and we, one of our pillars. Unfortunately, his parents died and he was adopted by a kind man who was a carpenter. It was there where he learnt the basics of carpentry. Realizing his talent, his father sent him to Jaipur to work with a relative who had worked in the royal palace. It was there where he honed his skills and became one of the finest carpenters. But he was a maverick like Correa. He was offered several lucrative assignments by top notch companies, but he refused. He couldn't be tied to one place. He was a free bird. Like his kind relative, he imported some of his young nephews from his village and taught them the skill. Soon he had a formidable team which could take up large contracts and give kick ass competiton.

Ram Bharose was a much married man. He was a Manglik which in astrological terms meant that the Mars in his horoscope was inauspicious. That would happen if the Mars was in the 2nd, 4th, 7th 8th or 12th house of the horoscope. In simpler terms it meant that no wife of his would survive. Whoever married him would die. He tried twice. Both the times the poor wife couldn't survive the bad positioning of Mars. The third time the local priest advised him to marry someone who herself was a Manglik. Luckily it worked. Now he was the father of three children. They were living in a small obscure village. But that had not stopped Ram Bharose from dreaming big. He intended to send them to an English-medium school. He was obsessed with computers and wanted to buy one for his children. In his opinion anyone who could operate a computer would be a successful man. I hated to shatter his dream and tell him that there were hundreds of zombies on Facebook who are doing their best to prove him otherwise. He was saving money to buy the ultimate tool that would take his children out of their village and their misery.

Ram Bharose respected talent and so did Correa. They immediately formed a mutual admiration society.

As our Pizza-Corner was slowly taking shape, there was this small hitch of choosing a location and oh yes, arranging the finances. But planning was never our strong point. Correa gave us strength. He told us it is not unusual. He had worked for big business houses and he told us that what happens there is unbelievably stupid and that we were not even half as crazy as they are.

We tried to get loan from banks but, as expected, failed. The banks were not impressed that I had worked abroad and made some money there. The important thing was that we didn't have experience in that field. Besides, our documentation was atrocious. We decided to discuss it with our respective parents. But our parents had never much involved themselves in our lives. We had their tacit support that was all. Finally we found a solution. That solution came from our Man Friday. Correa suggested that we were amateurs and wouldn't be able to handle the sharks in the banks. We needed a skilled negotiator who could not only present our case well but also be able to grease their palm. We had tried it once and were promptly thrown out of the manager's cabin. We learnt later that manager's were careful and didn't take bribes from any Tom, Dick or Harry for fear of being caught in the anti-corruption net.

Corruption is a double-edged sword. Sometimes it can land you in trouble too. While we officially don't condone it, the truth is that nothing works in this country without greasing palms and so, like a true Indian, we do not have any principled stand on not paying bribes. Every Indian grows up bribing someone, right from the TTE to book a berth in the train to the lab assistant in the Biology class to book a berth in the next class. So we didn't really have any qualms about paying bribe. Correa suggested three names. We decided to visit all three of them. We even invited Correa to come along with us. But he had his principles. He didn't interfere in anyone's personal business. So we decided to go ourselves. Mr. Keshav Gupta was third on the list and had the least impressive credentials. But after we met all the three we could only think of one name. Keshav Gupta. One small incident changed our opinion about him. Later Correa told us he had wanted to suggest Mr. Gupta. But he wanted us to decide for ourselves and hence gave two more options. We congratulated ourselves on being so intelligent.

Mr. Keshav Gupta's expertise was in arranging finances. He had a vast portfolio – right from students going abroad for higher studies to companies manufacturing solar panels. Gupta was a huge football fan. He supported Manchester United. In his profession too, he applied some principles of football. If you can't tackle the ball, tackle the player instead. He had a reputation of being very good in it. We didn't know how good he was as an accountant, but he was smart otherwise. We realized that on our second visit.

We were discussing our project when his secretary stormed in. She looked visibly agitated. Gupta was annoyed but maintained a facade of civility. 'Hi Julie. Looks as if the intercom has failed again.' Julie hesitated for a moment looking at us, 'No sir, I wanted to talk to you in private.' We both stood up to leave but Mr. Gupta bade us to keep sitting. 'Oh, they are old friends. Now what is it that couldn't wait?'

'It's about Ramesh, Sir.'

Ramesh was the office boy, we learnt later. 'He doesn't listen to me and is very rude.' Mr. Gupta waved his hand regally and said in a very sweet saccharine tone, 'Darling Julie, how many times have I told you. You and I, we are management whereas Ramesh is a servant. He is a small fry. I can fire him this very moment. But you will agree that getting servants is not easy. Besides, he is honest. We have to manage him. You are a smart girl.' Julie looked pleased at being called 'management'. She promised that the next time she would ignore his barbs. He swore silently as she left. Ramesh felt threatened to see Julie going inside Gupta's cabin. He was not a fool. He knew the office protocol. Julie seldom left the switchboard. He had to salvage the situation. So immediately he came into Gupta's cabin with his bag of complaints. Again Mr. Gupta regally waved his hand, 'Ramesh, who is Julie? She is just a two penny prostitute. But you?' He pointed a podgy finger at him and waited for impact. 'You are my right hand man. I can fire her this very moment. But you know getting an experienced secretary is not easy. Besides, you will agree, she is good in her work.' Ramesh looked pleased as punch and promised that he would ignore her henceforth. Mr. Gupta swore softly once again as he left.

We were highly impressed. Here was a true master. He had just delivered an Oscar winning performance. He killed two birds with one stone and yet no one was killed. If he cannot handle the bank managers, no one can.

Mr. Gupta was an avid *paan* (betel leaf) chewer. He kept a spittoon in his otherwise posh office and kept spitting out a red stream of spit into it every now and then. He had remarkable accuracy. His aim seldom missed the target. Once I tried to change the position of the spittoon when he turned his back on us. But soon as he returned from the shelf with his book, he noticed the displacement and reset it. We doffed our invisible hat to him in respect.

He considered himself a literary buff. His library proudly displayed several books of eminent writers. We had to suffer his literary sparks often. When asked what should be the size of our project, he would remark, 'I always say, it is not the size of the canvas but the stroke of the brush that creates a masterpiece'. Nachiket often asked him if he had read 'The Thief of Baghdad'. He was indeed a thief if one saw his fees.

But he was an expert at manipulation. He would create fake bank accounts and show the financial health as required by the bank. It wasn't as if the banks were not aware of it, but this was business. There were no scruples involved. The banks were happy as long as their palms were greased and the documents looked proper. We had failed on both the accounts. We didn't know how to prepare the documents and we were no good in bribing either.

Mr. Gupta was an influential man. He had made quite a name for himself in the banking circles and most of the bank managers were at his beck and call. So this time instead of us attending the meeting in formals, it was the other way round. This bank manager who was roaring like a lion the other day and had thrown us out of the bank was now purring like a cat. But we do not have a single mean bone. We promised ourselves to forgive him as soon as we received our first installment. Dad was proud of us that we had managed on our own.

One day, just as we were coming out of the CA's office, Mr. Gupta warned us that since the ovens and some of the other equipment were imports from USA, we would need an expert. Without a murmur, we accepted his recommendation. We knew that the consultant's consultancy fees would include his 'cut'. But we readily agreed as we knew our limitations. We would otherwise end up spending more money than his fees and yet not be able to manage. Besides, Gupta was a veteran in the field. At least we wouldn't have to check the consultant's credentials.

When Mr. Gupta asked us where would we open our Pizza-Corner, we just gaped. We hadn't thought about it. But he looked totally unfazed. He was a wise old man. He had seen all kinds of jerks. In fact, the bigger the jerks, the happier he was. When he invited us to The Club for a drink, we understood that we were one of his biggest catch. He was going to suck us dry like a sponge.

However, God has his own style of working. I am not an overtly devout person. But I have faith in him. My mother is a very religious woman. So we have a very religious atmosphere at home. I inherited it, you can say, through osmosis. He proved it that night. What giveth, will definitely cometh. That was the Lord's command.

As we sat on the elegantly manicured lawns of the posh club, two rookies with the master sipping scotch, the master looked totally in command. This was his stage. We were totally awed. But being awed is no buffer for being bored. This man could make coffee go to sleep!

We listened to his rambling's about how to do business and how to live life in general. We had traveled that lane before and knew what to expect. This was sheer murder. He had killed the night with his monologue. The only respite we got was when he frequented the washroom to spit. We thanked his betel chewing habit for once.

The scotch and our awkwardness had totally relaxed him and he had now dropped his guard. He was on a verbal diarrhea. We now knew about his academic accomplishments, his homely multi-talented wife, who was his prize trophy, and all his professional accomplishments. I glanced at Nachiket. He looked like he would fall off to sleep any moment. He could handle any amount of booze, but not this torture. Mr. Gupta was a silent killer.

Suddenly the club was engulfed in darkness. There was a power outage. It took a moment before the generator was switched on with a huge noise. There was a big spark in one of the wires and the power went off again. Probably that spark acted as a catalyst and the unthinkable happened. While the club went suddenly dark, Mr. Gupta sparkled. It wasn't that he suddenly discovered any great power of oratory, but he was speaking about something that we always loved to hear – girls. He said he had a daughter studying in a place called Manipal. It surprised me that why a rich bloke like him sent his only daughter to a remote place in Sikkim. Very soon I realized that I was wrong as usual. Manipal was a top educational hub in Karnataka. I wasn't embarrassed. Geography has never been my strong point!

We were all ears now. Every word uttered by him was Gospel.

He said that he had to go to Manipal to bring her home for her cousin's engagement. They were a joint family we learnt and this cousin was the second son of Mr. Gupta's younger brother. But he was too tied up at the moment and his office boy was also on leave. So he wasn't sure what to do. My friend and I exchanged glances. Suddenly all his ramblings was like music. We saw opportunity knocking. This was our territory. His daughter! Now where the hell was Manipal. But who cared. I just had a moment's doubt though. Mr. Gupta was a rotund, ugly man. Would the girl be a chip of the old block? But I quashed the thought immediately. 'Be Positive. Be positive.' My school Principal's exhortation finally found utterance.

Nachu and I may have diverse views on a plethora of issues, but there were some situations where we didn't need any prompting. Almost simultaneously, we both brought in our most solemn expression. 'Sir, we are busy no doubt. But not as busy as you are. We would like to help. Our mothers have taught us that we should help people in distress.' (Our mothers would have been shocked and surprised to hear this as we hardly ever listened to what they said.) Mr. Gupta looked pleased as punch. Bringing his little girl escorted by these two lovely boys was like bringing her in an armored truck. They were so young and so dumb. His little girl would be safe with them.

We wrangled an invitation to the Gupta residence for breakfast next morning for the final drill before the departure.

✦

It was a sprawling double storied bungalow which was not surprising, looking at the money he made. It had that nice old fashioned look which meant that he hadn't created this wealth. His father loaned money on interest, we were told. So sucking the blood of innocent victims was an old family tradition!

We removed our shoes outside and sat in his elegant drawing room when his wife came in like a caparisoned elephant. She was decked in more jewellery than the whole store of Mussaddilal Jewelers. She wore a bright blue sari with her head covered with the corner of the sari which she kept adjusting. Our heads crashed as we both bent down to touch her feet. Her face shone with undisguised pleasure. 'In today's world it is hard to find such boys. Full credit to your parents for bringing you up so well,' she gushed. We sat there pretending to be totally innocent. Her husband was doubly pleased and looked at with that avuncular pleased look that we had finally given him something that his wife finally found worth approving.

A giant plasma TV dominated one wall. He proudly switched it on. Immediately Rahul Gandhi's huge image assaulted us. He guffawed loudly, 'When Rahul Gandhi is on TV, it means it is election time.' News bored me. I would rather watch monkeys masturbating in the zoo than watching these hucksters. They all showed the same news and each claimed that it was "breaking news" exclusively on their channel.

I looked at Mr. Gupta. When not joking he was a bore. But now he seemed even a bigger bore. His jokes were bland, political and as the American children say, 'so gay'. It was in the US that I learnt that gay need not necessarily relate to sexuality. Anything boring could be termed gay.

Even at the best of times my concentration level is low. Now it was bare minimum. My eyes started wandering.

From where we sat I could see a huge courtyard in the centre surrounded by rooms.

An old lady sat in the corner of the courtyard washing utensils. The tap was running unabated, no one bothering that a natural resource was going waste. But then it wasn't surprising in a country where the rich treat themselves as royalty.

There were servants everywhere. By now we knew the count in the Gupta household. The servants clearly outnumbered the portly family whom we were shortly going to meet. But most of the servants looked old, perhaps an indication that they had served long enough in this household to consider it their home. I looked with a new respect at Mr. Gupta.

My thought process was abruptly interrupted by a man who came in and announced that breakfast was ready.

Mr. Gupta led us to the dining room laughing uproariously at his own silly jokes. My ears had already gone deaf. I had forgotten why he was laughing.

As we entered the room and surveyed the table, we gasped.

At least one thing was certain. Mr. Gupta would never be our customer. On the table was a huge spread of all possible Indian delicacies and yet the servants kept carrying a posse of food. It looked like a set in BBC's 'Flavors of India' show.

I couldn't believe my eyes that anyone could eat this many things for breakfast. There were samosas, kachoris, an assortment of sweets, dahi-vadas, parathas right from the plain ones to the generously filled aloo and gobi parathas. I swallowed hard. Each dish was dripping with ghee, screaming of cholesterol. For the plain parathas, there were bowls of curries and yoghurt.

Mrs. Gupta stood there beaming and enquiring anxiously if there was something that was left out. Mr. Gupta gave one of his throaty laughs and said something silly. I didn't even bother to be polite.

The servants stood behind, one for each of us. They had been given instructions to see that our plates were never even half empty. I was gobbling up the food so that we could leave the place soon. But the moment I picked up something it was promptly refurbished. I was thinking of how to wriggle out of the situation when Nachiket hissed into my ears 'Heimlich maneuver'.

I was horrified.

'Nachu, these guys are vegetarians. We must respect their culture. You can eat whatever you want to later.' Nachu was a devout vegetarian in the US but turned into a carnivore once in India.

He nudged me hard in my stomach, his eyes fixed on Mr. Gupta. Mr. Gupta's eyes looked like they would pop out of their sockets. He was choking on a large chunk of kachori. I felt a sadistic pleasure. At least now he would never laugh and eat together. But Heimlich maneuver! I had no idea. How I wished I had been more sincere in the first aid class.

Nachiket jumped, spilling water in his food. I think it was deliberate. He swore later that it was an accident but I don't believe it. He went behind Mr. Gupta, grasped his large belly and gave him a big upward jerk. Nothing happened. He kept sweating and going red.

Nachu once again tried the maneuver, a little harder this time. The piece of food stuck inside flew out like a missile and fell on a plate. Mrs. Gupta, who was weeping till now was howling. We had saved her *suhaag* (her portly husband).

I promised myself I wouldn't flirt with someone who was even a distant relative of theirs. Little did I know that we had encountered a family of chokers. Soon we would have to use the Heimlich maneuver again. This time to his daughter.

As we were leaving the Gupta household with a few extra calories and dozens of books, which I was sure Avantika, his daughter, would never read and dozens of emotions that would take a long time to forget, Mrs. Gupta pushed an envelope in my hand, as her husband looked benevolently but with lesser energy. I asked her what it was.

She said that now that we were family her husband couldn't accept any fees.

We just stared at her. We Indians are very emotional people. We build long time relations even while traveling short distance in a bus. The same fellow traveler who could have taken your life for a seat wouldn't hesitate to sacrifice his life once that friendship is cemented over a cup of sugary tea at a roadside stall near the bus stop.

But this was different. I felt tears well up in my eyes. Money always did that to me.

Mrs. Gupta ordered us that from now on we must call her Aunty and Mr. Gupta, Uncle. We could have called them Mummy and Daddy!

Nachu and I once again banged our heads against each other as we bent down to touch her feet. Long back as part of our school project I had gone to see the process of shoe making. They used a process called 'tawing' to soften the leather. I felt that money had just tawed our souls. But we too had our morals. We expected that Avantika would be as roly poly as her parents and we felt a surge of affection towards her.

Sister Avantika, your brothers are on their way!

While returning from Gupta Mansion, we were wrapped up in our thoughts. It had been a very eventful morning. A thought crossed my mind. In a country used to eating THAT kind of food, would it make sense to open a pizzeria?

Without intending to, Mr. Gupta had touched our deepest fears.

While waiting for the feast, we were watching television. Rahul Gandhi, the scion of the Congress Empire, was sitting on the floor and eating in a Dalit's house. It didn't bother us. Politicians use all kind of dirty tricks during elections. But what stopped us to ponder was Mr. Gupta's comment. 'Can't blame that poor sod. After all who can eat bland pasta everyday?' He guffawed.

We laughed politely but he had touched our innermost fears. The country can accept Sonia Gandhi. But will they accept pizzas and pastas?

✦ ✦ ✦

III

MANIPAL – where it is normal to be WEIRD

As we walked out of the Baijal Airport, we both looked around, Nachiket to charge his mobile and me to charge myself. God created human beings. Human being created mobiles. Both needed regular recharging. God didn't make any charger for his creation but gave humans the brains to do so. We called it beer. Baijal Airport was disappointing.

We both came back empty handed. Angrily we seated ourselves in a cab.

The roads were narrow, un-metalled and dusty. We stared dully outside. If Manipal was going to be anything like this we were doomed. We promised ourselves that we shall leave immediately with Avantika. Now even Avantika no longer attracted us. Angrily.

I suggested we call Avantika and let her know that we had come.

Avantika did not pick up the phone. Suddenly it occurred to us that she may be in the class. So we sent her an SMS and got an immediate reply. 'Pick me up from Sutta Point.' Where the hell was that? We received another SMS. 'Gimme a call once you reach TC. Timmy's may be more convenient.'

What language did this moron speak? I couldn't make head or tail of it! Nachiket was least interested. His eyes were roving. Finally he spotted a tacky roadside bar. As we were debating about should whether to go in or not, suddenly without intimation, there was a peal of thunder and it began raining. We decided we had no option. It was now pouring. We weren't sure when we would find the next bar. We braced ourselves, opened the car door and ran inside before we could get wet. There was a big ditch right in front of the bar which was now a pool. It wasn't that large. But just as Nachiket tried to jump across it, he slipped and fell in the ditch. He was furious. I was wearing Bermuda shorts. So I could jump effortlessly and crossed with a thud. A spray of mud decorated my back side. We entered the bar wet and muddy. The bar was nothing but a shanty with some wooden chairs. There were hundreds of flies sitting on the wet and sticky tables. There was a huge din inside but suddenly it became quiet for a moment as we entered.

The Chinese describe health as a balance between Yin and Yang. I do not know about my Yin. But my Yang was definitely beer. We had to keep that balance by seeing that we were never short of Yang. A few drops of the elixir and our mood lifted. The bar didn't look tacky any more. The owner and his staff seemed like angels. They were simple folks. They could feel our discomfiture and were trying to make us as much comfortable as possible. I was ashamed. We were not snooty. It was just the thirst. We now showed our gratitude by pretending we were enjoying. We smiled at everyone making them still more uncomfortable. After two beers, we signaled for the bill and as we were leaving, we left a generous tip. The owner, delighted with our generosity came to see us off right till the entrance. Our spirits lifted and our moods restored, we again embarked on mission Avantika.

I looked out of the window. The rains had washed off all the dirt and the road had a new washed look. The change in the landscape was both dramatic and magical. We had never seen so much greenery. We were now driving across a bridge. The sparkling water under the bridge was flowing in full abundance. There were huge banana groves. Tall and majestic coconut trees lined the roads.

The harshness of the sun had gone taking away all our harshness too. Our hearts were now dancing like peacocks. Suddenly Nachiket started singing loudly. He couldn't sing to save his life. We had taken out a towel to dry ourselves. I tried to stuff it into his mouth. His arms and legs were flaying everywhere as he tried to duck the now dirty towel. Laughing and joking, we entered Udupi, the temple town.

The calm driver suddenly looked like he was going to have an orgasm. He was from Udupi and was mighty proud about it. The Krishna temple here was unique in the country, he explained, in that the lord faces the west whereas everywhere he faces the east. He further explained that legend has it that a devotee named Kanakadesa was not allowed entry inside since he belonged to a lower caste. Undeterred, he sat on the western side of the temple praying. The lord, pleased with his devotion, turned around, broke the wall and gave him darshan through a window. Even now the devotees can see

Lord Krishna only through this window, which is exquisitely carved and silver plated and named Kanakana Kindi after the devotee. Absentmindedly we promised we would visit it before leaving.

As we entered Manipal, we decided to first check into a hotel and freshen up before meeting Avantika. The first impression had to be good.

Manipal, we found, was a libertine's paradise. God and the founders of this university combined together to produce this absolute genius of symbiotic creation. Each square meter of land screamed Carpe Diem.

Surrounded by beaches and amidst lush greenery this small educational town was like a pearl in a oyster hidden from the world because of its geography.

The place attracted as many attractive birds of various species as it did students from all over the world. One had to be a keen bird watcher to spot birds. But no problem with girls. They were there everywhere.

The hotel owner was weak in Hindi but that was not an impediment for a raconteur of his caliber. After a few pegs, his fluency in Hindi increased. He gave us a hilarious picture post of this place.

He explained that Manipal (which he pronounced as Moneypal. How true!) was the haven of rich men's bored brood. This place offered everything necessary for growing children. Drugs, booze, sex and if one were lucky, a very good degree. We laughed till our stomach hurt.

Manipal had no taboos. We loved the place. In three days I was proposed by at least four girls and three boys. A foreigner tried to sell her camera to me for magic mushroom and another was willing to sleep with Nachu for grass. I knew about grass but it was there where I learnt that mushroom was not a vegetable.

There was no ban on drinking in the open. It was common to see students drinking openly in the streets even in the noon without being harassed by cops. It was rumored that the owners of the college paid a huge amount to the police to keep their hands off them. If that was indeed true, my respect for them grew. I raised a toast for them. In short Manipal was, well, Manipal. I find myself inadequate to take up that arduous task of describing Manipal!. I have always believed that originality is a myth. The only original creations have been Adam and Eve. So without a tinge of guilt, I borrow a couplet from Dad's collection of Ghazals:

Gar Firdaus bar rue zamin ast,
hami asto, hami asto, hami asto.

[If there is a Paradise anywhere on earth,
it's here! it's here! it's here!]

Before I continue with my story, we wish to put on record our sincere gratitude to the venerable Mr. Gupta.

Without him we wouldn't have known that such a place existed in India.

✦

Manipal got its name from the local word Manu meaning mud and Palla meaning lake. We had seen enough of the mud and seen one Palla.

It took us exactly twenty minutes to see the whole town and another twenty minutes to acquaint ourselves with the acronyms. To survive in Manipal, one had to acquaint himself with them. Without getting acquainted one would feel that the denizens were speaking in an alien language. I soon learnt that KC was Kamath Circle and TC was Tiger Circle. Sutta Point was nothing but a kiosk selling cigarettes and snacks. Timmy's was a small shack on the eastern side of the hostel blocks where the lazy boys of the 9th Block went to fill their stomach when their legs were unwilling to walk that extra mile to eat something fulfilling.

The driver cursed us when we went to pick Avantika there. The road was narrow, unmetalled, uphill and undulating. I was glad that I had spotted a bar while going. Little did I know then that the last thing you worried about in Manipal were bars. The place was teeming with bars. You didn't search them, they searched you out!

But as soon as we reached up, his frustration forgotten, our driver giggled. There standing near the shanty was a row of stylishly dressed pretty girls and a few boys. Looked like Avantika had brought her entire class there. This was going to be a logistic nightmare.

How would they all fit in?

We were cheerfully ordered to make several trips. This time the driver wasn't cursing. I think he had breathed in the air of Manipal and now was a game for anything.

We looked at the girls. They came in all shapes and sizes. There were two delightful plump girls. Nachiket looked at me for a moment and nodded. We were sure that one of the two girls must be Avantika. The whole group sniggered. Avantika wasn't one of them. Our jaws dropped as a stunning girl in shorts came forward.

We could never have dreamt that Avantika was slim, doe eyed, dusky and had a very cheerful smile. Mrs. Gupta had given birth to the eighth wonder!

I wasn't very old. Neither could I claim to have seen many surprises in life. But I can say it with confidence that whatever little I had seen, this one topped them all.

Nachiket looked to me like he needed his famed Heimlich maneuver.

The driver looked enquiringly at me and asked where we would like to go.

'DT' they screamed in unison.

We may not know where the famous Krishna temple was yet. But we had done our homework about the pubs.

DT was the spot. If one compared it with the larger cities, there was nothing extraordinary about it. But Manipal was not because of its bricks and mortars. The students had an amazing vibrancy. It was they who made Manipal what it was.

Manipal was dotted with points. There was Student's Point, Sutta Point, Parotha Point, even a Suicide Point and the breathtaking End Point. I remember the precise moment when we decided to open our restaurant there. We were standing at End Point, smoking a joint and trying to devour the amazingly scenic beauty with our eyes. We had beer cans in our hands.

Nachiket raised his can and said, 'Standing here I feel like I am the Don of this city. I am the Emperor and this is my kingdom.' Avantika's friends cheered lustily. By now we had got used to moving in a caravan. We called it the Avantika entourage.

In that moment of hallucinatory madness, I imagined our little pizzeria in Manipal was born. I even gave a little speech about the size of the canvas should be greater than the length of the brush to make it a master. Luckily they were as stoned as me and no one cared what I said. Avantika's friends lifted both of us on their shoulders and airlifted us to the car.

One nerdy guy with an oversized pair of glasses suggested that maybe tomorrow would be late and there wouldn't be any shop available for rent so let's search for a place now. Unsurprisingly he was cheered lustily. They cheered anything and everything. In fact cheering seemed their third most popular activity; the first being smoking and second drinking.

The next day I woke up with a huge hangover. It seemed like the globe was suddenly reminded that it was rotating very slowly and had to make up the lost time. It took a spin. I held the chair to control myself. Nachiket was snoring. He was lying half on the cot and half on the floor. My hands were shaking as I lighted a cigarette and ordered a cup of hot black coffee. I decided I would never drink again.

The black coffee seemed to clear some of the fog. I ordered another cup. As I was having my second cup, I felt I was signing a cheque. Terrified, I dived for my bag and checked my cheque book. This time I rushed to the toilet and retched my guts out.

I had issued a cheque of one lakh to one Mr. Shenoy. In the details, I had scrawled as advance towards store rent.

Strangely only that part was a blur. The rest of the evening I remembered with amazing clarity. In one of the paradoxes of my life, I always seemed to forget the important things. But the unimportant ones stuck with photographic memory. The whole evening swam before my eyes like a movie. I remembered going into the blue water. The tequila competition. The wild dancing. Then hopping to sky lounge. Then back to the hotel. Smoking. The nerd commenting that the effect of weed is heightened by sweets. We all trooping into 'Crumbs'.

A smile creased my face. When I thought about it, I couldn't stop smiling. Suddenly the one lakh advance didn't seem very important.

It had happened in the wee hours of the morning. We were tired and drunk. Half the guys had already passed out. The rest were sitting on the pavement having one more beer. Suddenly Avantika turned to me and kissed me on my lips gently. I immediately responded back. There was passion in it but no lust. It was a slow languorous kiss. Warm and gentle. Soft and silky. My hands reached around her shoulders and took her in a gentle hug. I could feel her warm breath on my neck as she settled herself comfortably close to me.

I had to look up because of the way she was sitting. A thousand stars sparkled like tiny diamonds winking mischievously at me. It was a serene evening. Cool fresh breeze kissed our cheeks nodding its approval. There was no music. The night was delightfully silent. But when you are in love, no music is required. We created our own symphony that only we played and we heard.

We were sitting like that even when the night crossed the threshold and the dawn arrived blushing like a newly-wed.

I do not know when this beautiful dream ended and the harsh ugly hangover took over. If only I had drunk a little less!

✦

Nachiket woke up strangely cheerful and looking fresh. He had scored with his mushroom chick once again. Nothing else could be more important.

When I asked him about the signing amount, he was totally ignorant. Nachiket was the guy who had accused me that I thought with my dick!

Many months later, a group of school boys visited our store and one of them had looked at me with unmitigated adoration and confessed that I was a role model for him. He asked me about how I took such a bold decision to come to a new city and start a business. I had to cook up a story about vision, courage and foresight.

How could we tell those innocent kids that we hadn't taken even a single right decision when we were sober! We couldn't be role model for anyone even to save our life. Our life was one roller coaster ride. We ourselves didn't know when we would be on the top and when we would have a free fall. The chances of fall were always more.

Full credit to Avantika's friends. They had helped us select one of the most breathtaking spots in Manipal. The place was surrounded by lush green forest which looked like it was designed by a landscapist. Nachiket wanted to later expand the place with romantic separate booths for couples. I reined in his imagination. The nerdy guy had visualized the interiors. He wanted to name it Poison and have the Gods of Rock in there. I had to remind him that we were going to sell pizza. He asked can't you make it a combo? Something like Pizza with Hookah? I congratulated him on his deep understanding and on his business acumen and didn't give it another thought. He was, however, pleased as punch. Another guy, not to be outdone, asked if grass would be allowed. I patiently told him that we will consider.

Manipal now had a special place in my heart. I did not know whether we would be successful in our business, but my heart now was here. Avantika was my love. She would be here for at least two years.

It was time to leave. Avantika, Nachiket and I bid the others goodbye. By now Nachiket came to know about us and teased us no end. But Avantika was a good sport. Manipal had us in its throes. We had come to Manipal hating it so much that we wanted to leave as soon as possible. Now we were leaving with a heavy heart, although it was only for a short while.

The Guptas were evidently pleased to see their daughter. We were treated like royalty. But with our past experience, we politely declined the offer of breakfast but couldn't say no to coffee. The Guptas were great hosts. Even the coffee arrived with the inevitable samosas and sweets. The only thing missing were the parathas. We were hungry but not for this kind of breakfast. Avantika had a naughty grin on her face. She soon returned with fresh sandwiches and toasts. In the meanwhile, Gupta dropped a bomb. The bank had declined the loan. We thought it was his revenge for declining breakfast. I picked up a samosa and signaled Nachiket to do the same. But that didn't change anything. Nachiket, true to his wont, dipped the kachori in the syrup of jalebi and ate nonchalantly. We explained to Mr. Gupta about our decision to open a pizza shop in Manipal. He was pleased that at least we had decided on the location. We had brought pictures of the shop location. He seemed pleased with the location. He advised us to go ahead and prepare the interior drawings. But we were not making any headway.

Finally Mr. Gupta decided to meet our parents. We all had a luncheon meeting in a five star hotel. Mr. Gupta came with a fresh business plan. He had cleverly included a market report on the viability of Manipal as the perfect location for the project. Our parents were pleased at our business acumen. Nachiket and I looked at each other with a look of modesty.

Gupta suggested that perhaps dad and uncle could come along with us. The banks would be reassured to see mature men involved in the project. But both vehemently opposed the idea. They said that it was not their project and it was only apt that we went ourselves to the bank. But they were willing to become guarantors. Mr. Gupta too agreed. Nachiket's father was a businessman. He understood how the system worked. He suggested that we could offer collateral security. My father too agreed. We stared dumbly but didn't bother to ask anything. Mr. Gupta thought for some time and then declared that the bank should have no problem in releasing the money. I wanted to know if we would still have to bribe the bank manager. But sometimes it pays to be silent.

After the meeting, Nachu's father invited us for a drink in the Club. We were following Nachu's car. Dad and I were silent in the car wrapped in our thoughts. I didn't know how to begin. 'Dad, Thanks.' Dad just looked at me and grinned.

'Your mom will be happy. You are finally learning your etiquettes'. I laughed. Mother had a hard time taming her wild son. She would visit swamijis, tantriks and astrologers. *Vibhutis* or sacred ash was applied on my resisting head which I would wipe off angrily, black threads were tied around my wrist to ward off evil which immediately found their way out through the window. A new tutor arrived every week. Dad surveyed the posse of tutors coming and going unperturbed. He was unruffled. Folding his newspaper, he used to gently rebuke mom to be patient.

Once a lady tutor with intimidating testimonials was hired. She was a disciplinarian and very easy with her cane. I got caned at least once every day. But one day I lost my patience. I had come back from school with my report card. I had failed in Mathematics. Worse, I had picked up a fight in the bus while returning from school and had been nicked. Fighting was common, losing wasn't. I was in a real surly mood. The moment she caned me, I snatched the cane from her hand and started caning her mercilessly.

She screamed and ran out of the room, me running behind her. Mom was shocked to see the disheveled sight of that woman. The next week I was sent to a boarding school. The boarding school packed me back within a month informing my parents that I was unteachable. Finally I settled down in Bishop Cotton School and somehow completed my schooling.

My face was crimson as dad teased me about that time. A lot of beer had flowed down the bridges. I sheepishly said so. Dad smiled and looked at me indulgently. He had stood by me in all my battles and it was a miracle that he still believed in me. Perhaps that was the power of love.

Normally in any husband-wife relationship there is one dominant partner. Not so in my parent's case. They both were very docile. It was a miracle that I had any competitive bone in my body. I had been bullied, abused, beaten and suffered a hundred things. The thesaurus would fail in finding the words. But in a way it helped me to harden up for the tougher battles that lay ahead of me as an adult though I didn't take it as kindly then. When at thirteen I was sent to a hostel for two years, it is where I mutated. Within the next six months of my return from the hostel, I took revenge on all my perpetrators. The prey had now become the predator!

Nachu's car took a turn. I knew the way. We were almost there. Dad suddenly turn towards me and said, 'Teju. Why don't you go to Rajmundhry tomorrow?'

Rajmundhry? Where the hell was that? And why all of a sudden?

We were entering the club. 'We can discuss it later' but with a twinkle in his eyes he said, 'This is the season for some rare fish there. You will enjoy it.'

I loved fish. But this whole business sounded fishy. Why was I suddenly being sent to Rajhmundry?

✦ ✦ ✦

IV

Tricked to learn
BUSINESS TRICKS

Rajhmundry was a small business town located about three hundred miles east of Hyderabad. We entered the city via a beautiful bridge built on the large and prosperous Godavari River. Andhra Pradesh derives much of its prosperity from this area. Majority of the big businesses and industries in the state could find their genesis in this basin.

This area could rightly be called as the paper capital of the south. There were a lot of mini paper mills dotting the landscape.

The air smelt of fish and salt water as I walked out of the hotel. The hotel belonged to one of dad's friend. He had sent an envelope which he wanted me to deliver it to him personally. Mr. Gangadhar was an elderly man with a very distinguished look. He was tall and stood very straight and always wore a snow white dhoti and shirt. He was pleased to see me and told me that we shall be eating lunch in his home.

He wouldn't listen to my protests. On the way he stopped at a large fast food joint. He said he had just a few minutes work there. The joint looked like a cross between KFC, McDonald and Pizza Hut. He instructed the driver to keep the air conditioner on for me.

He walked a few steps and as if on second thoughts he came back and said, 'Mr. Tejas, it is very hot outside, why don't you come in.' I jumped at the invitation. I had been dying to see a proper joint just to see how they run it.

The owner was not available but the manager knew Mr. Gangadhar well. He was extremely deferential to him. We were offered a seat. After waiting for about ten minutes, Mr. Gangadhar asked if I would like to see the place. I readily agreed. The manager took us on a conducted tour of the place. I saw everything with great interest and asked him several questions. Before we realized it was more than two hours when we got out of the joint.

Mr. Gangadhar lived in a huge mansion. It wasn't surprising since he was the owner of a hotel. As we entered his house, a servant came running. He seated me in a comfortable sofa as Mr. Gangadhar excused himself to freshen up. His wife meanwhile came to greet me. I stood up and folded my hands, 'Namaste madam.' She smiled broadly and explained in halting Hindi that she wasn't fluent in English or Hindi. I assured her it was no problem. She smiled again and went back. Shortly afterwards the servant led me to the dining room.

I looked hungrily at the table. The food laid on it was fit for a king – a variety of fish, crabs, prawns, chicken and what not.

In south India, food is served by the women of the house. It is considered rude if servants serve your food. As the lady started serving, the aroma wafting out of the hot dishes made me ravenous. Andhra cooking is a very elaborate affair. But it is not for the weak stomached. The food is extremely spicy. After the fish, she served steaming hot rice and ghee. Mr. Gangadhar asked me to begin.

I noticed that there were no spoons. Andhraites love to eat with their hands. I took the cue from Mr. Gangadhar and dug into the food. It was delicious.

The lady was delighted to see me enjoying the food. Mr. Gangadhar was a delightful host. He explained about each dish as we ate.

'This is Pulasa fish. Known as the queen of fish, it is a rare fish, found only in the months of June and July. Teju, do you know each fish is sold for two thousand rupees.' My eyes popped out. I tried it again. His wife laughed. It was really delicious. I noticed that Mr. Gangadhar had casually started calling me Teju.

'She cooked it yesterday itself after your father informed us about your visit. This particular fish tastes better if it is cooked a day before its eaten up.' I felt embarrassed and mumbled that there was no need to purchase such an expensive fish for me.

He laughed gently and said that he was not sure if we would ever meet again. Saying so he pointed to the next dish. 'This fish is known as the Cheera Meenu. It is so small that it escapes through an ordinary net and it so has to be caught in a saree. Hence it is called saree fish. It is also a very rare fish and its price depends on that day's catch.' Then suddenly his eyes twinkled mischievously. 'Sometimes it is good to have influence. I know the local fish market. So getting it is never a problem.' He chuckled.

It was a delightful lunch but it was debatable whether his narration was better than the meal. I had never enjoyed a meal so much. Just when I thought we had finished lunch, his wife came in with a trolley smiling. It was laden with plates and plates of mangoes of various mouthwatering varieties. I cursed myself for over eating. Mango is my favourite fruit. Had I known about it, I would have eaten less.

Mr. Gangadhar explained that he owned mango groves in the coastal belt and all these mangoes were from there. 'The coast grows more than two hundred and fifty varieties. We grow only ten.' He pointed at one, 'This is Banganapalli.' Then with his trademark twinkle he went on, 'smart marketing has made the Alphonso dubbed as the king of mangoes, but trust me, there is no mango which can match. Banganapalli. We south Indians always claim it as the king of mangoes.' I smiled. This old man was charming. I picked up one of the slices and scooped out the flesh. It was truly delicious. Both husband and wife were looking expectantly at me. I groaned in appreciation much to their delight. The mango was very succulent and had no fibre. I was having a gastronomic orgasm!

Next he turned to another one. 'This is called Suvarnarekha. The one next to is Neelum and then there is Totapari.' He went on explaining the salient features of each one of them. Each mango tasted different, each having its own individuality.

My hands and mouth were dripping with the nectar-like juice of the different mangoes. As the servant came with a bowl of water and towel, I realized that only I was eating the mangoes.

'Sir, I have noticed that no plate was placed for you. Don't you like mangoes?'

Mr. Gangadhar was silent for a while. Then he asked me if I had finished. We came to the living room to rest for a while before leaving for the hotel.

Then in a very low voice, he started. What he said was heart breaking. I rued my question. Eyes glazed and looking into nothingness, he described the most heart wrenching story I had heard in my short life.

His only son had died when his motorcycle crashed into a coming lorry killing him on the spot. I could feel the pain in the father's voice as he narrated how he saw his son's mangled head crushed under the lorry. It took the couple some time to get over the tragedy.

'Nihar loved mangoes' He said as we stood up to leave.

The next day I moved into their house from the hotel. Mrs. Gangadhar couldn't control her tears when I called her Amma and told her that I will stay in Nihar's room. I had gone there for a day but stayed on for a week instead.

We had a set routine. I was woken up in the morning with the rich and aromatic filter coffee Mrs. Gangadhar would personally bring. She woke up at five in the morning before any one else, would have an early shower and pray in her temple. Then she would set the coffee machine which was nothing but a set of two cylindrical cups, the top one with sieves in which she pressed freshly ground coffee and chickory and poured boiling water and allow the coffee to brew and collect at the bottom cylinder. Then she would start planning for the breakfast. The south Indian cuisine involves a lot of grinding. Rice, which is their staple food, is soaked overnight with some lentils and spices and ground into a paste to make delicious dosas and idlis. They also use a lot of spices and herbs which are ground into a paste before using them for cooking.

The lady, once having planned the menu for the day, would then order the servants to grind the masalas. Electrical grinders were not allowed in the house. It killed off the taste, she said. Once the servants began grinding, she would come and collect the freshly brewed coffee and then mix it with fresh milk and sugar and make a thick and aromatic coffee for drinking. It would be piping hot when she brought it to me everyday.

Mrs. Gangadhar loved flowers. She would weave them into a garland and then wear it on her hair. Her forehead would be smeared with the holy ash.

Once we had our coffee, we would get ready and come down for breakfast which would be either hot steaming idlis with a large varieties of chutneys and steaming sambhar or golden paper thin dosas served with delectable chutneys and sambhar. Sometimes she served *upma,* a samolina delicacy. This would be followed by another cup of her trademark coffee. I loved to inhale the overpowering smell of freshly brewed coffee.

Mr. Gangadhar would then drop me to his friend's fast food joint where I sat with the owner or the manager and observe how they worked. Later a car would be sent for me and I would go and explore the city. It was a small town with nothing much to do.

We would then go home for a sumptuous lunch. This would be followed by a little siesta and hot steaming coffee again. We would then go to the hotel. I would sneak into the bar for a couple of drinks and then head for dinner.

I was surprised that dad or mom showed no eagerness for me to return. Little did I know that I had been skillfully manipulated into an internship without any inkling. Three weather beaten oldies had tricked me into it. I didn't know Nachiket had been similarly tricked by his equally devious father.

After I returned from Rajmundhry, one day Avantika, Nachiket and I were sitting in the balcony of our house sipping mom's special panna made from raw mangoes. The mangoes were boiled and then the pulp was mixed with salt, sugar and mom's secret spices and diluted with ice cold water to make a delightful drink. Just then the phone rang. It was Mr. Gupta. Our loan had been sanctioned. We had to now start work in earnest. I rushed inside and informed my dad and then called Nachu's father to thank him for the support. He sounded delighted. He congratulated us and advised us to begin work. I was looking for mom. But she was already in her sanctum sanctorum thanking our deity for his kindness. Immediately afterwards she sent our servant to fetch sweets. We had crossed the first hurdle.

✦

Avantika informed us that she had to leave for Manipal. Suddenly we remembered that we had to execute the lease agreement. I offered to go to Manipal and sign it. Nachu winked at me. He knew why I was eager to go. Mr. Gupta had now won the approval of our parents. He had now become our full time advisor. He advised us to split our responsibilities. We now learnt to ignore his wisecracks and his silly sense of humor and his constant spitting.

Avantika and I packed our stuff and left for Manipal the next day.

Mr. Shenoy had a very professionally done agreement which we sent to Mr. Gupta. He sent it to his lawyer. Once satisfied, he called me to go ahead with the signing. We were now officially the owners of the shop.

I realized that I could not go on living in the hotel. It was becoming too expensive. Now that we had signed the lease, we decided to rent an apartment.

Avantika's friends, once again, came to our rescue. It was decided that we carefully spend our money. I would be sharing their friend's apartment till Nachiket moved in. We could thus stretch each rupee.

Nikhil, Manya and Ajay had a three-bedroom apartment in the beautiful Emerald Heights. I was inducted as the fourth partner. I was naturally expected to give a house warming party. In other words, it was another excuse to paint the town red. These guys couldn't be satisfied sitting in one place.

We hopped from Poison to T-spirits to DT with intermittent intervals for rolling a joint. Finally we ate at a small Malaysian restaurant. Momos were their specialty and I loved momos. We had chicken teriyaki and noodles and some vegetables cooked in sauces.

Crumbs had a delightful array of confectionery and desserts.

As we were entering our apartment building, we saw four boys and a girl entering. The Nepali watchman was blissfully drunk and was stonily looking at the youngsters. The girl was drinking beer straight from the bottle which was three-fourth empty. Her friends were drinking whisky in some cheap plastic glasses. The watchman told them that he was a *bewda* (drunkard) and stonily asked them for a drink. The girl patronizingly wrapped her hand on his shoulder and told him that she had only one-fourth of the beer left. It wouldn't help him if he had only that much. But she would at least feel good if she finished it. Her friends were blunt and said, 'Saale, if we give you the drink, what shall we drink? GHANTA?'

Normally the watchman was very polite and stood up to greet. But tonight he was tired, sozzled and miffed to see all the drinks going in a procession right in front of him. It was like a bar on legs.

He looked through me and said condescendingly to no one in particular, *'Saala, hum piye to bewda* because I am drinking here in the open. But its ok if you guys drink behind the four walls. You will still be called a sahib. And that girl. If a poor girl does what she does, she's a prostitute! Mother fucking assholes.'

Our gang heartily agreed and said our good byes.

As we were entering the apartment, one of them imitated the watchman, *'Saala tum kare to romance, hum kare to sex.'* We all rolled on the floor laughing.

The nerd had a submission the next day and had politely excused himself from our party. Now he was upset to see us disturbing his tranquility. He requested all of us to make less noise. His other friends pinned him down on the floor and poured a quarter of the beer down his throat leaving him gagging and cursing.

Laughing all of us sprayed wherever we could find space.

As I was passing out, I thought of the poor Nepali watchman. I reached the fridge to see if there was anything there. I fished out two cans of beers and went to give him.

He had blissfully passed out. I returned back with the beers.

The management fired him a week later. We lost a bad watchman but a great entertainer.

The new watchman was a bore. But the management liked him because he was a stickler for rules.

He hated our midnight soirees.

I was running out of luck. Avantika's grandma slipped in the toilet and had broken her hip bone. She was admitted in the hospital. I understood how close her family was. They were a joint family after all. Needless to say, she had to miss some crucial classes and go and visit her grandma.

But as luck would have it, the old lady conked off even before Avantika had started. Now she wouldn't come back to Manipal till the thirteenth day ceremony which generally marks completion of the mourning period. I was feeling like an abandoned puppy!

✦

Last night exchanged some SMSs with Avantika. This has become regular after that passionate night.

'Wassup.'

'Nothing. Nothing at all. :P'

'You cheapster. How's work going?'

'Huh?'

'Forget it. When are you coming?'

'Already am. Just looking at your sms :P'

'Dirty boy. And here I am buying an expensive evening dress for a night out with you.'

'You know darling. While I was in the tub, a thought struck me. Why spend so much money on buying clothes when my biggest fantasy is to see you without them.'

'While you are in the tub, go play with yourself. I am too classy for you.'

Avantika is really classy. Wonder what good deed I had done in my last life to deserve her! She is my karma. I was definitely a far better person in last life.

SMSs can never be a substitute for the real world. I can no longer live without Avantika. Flight turns out to be very expensive. So I am taking a train instead.

Good bye Manipal. You are nothing to me without my Avantika.

✦

If I were asked to name the biggest sadist in the world, I would unhesitatingly say Dr. Martin Cooper. This guy has single handedly destroyed more homes by inventing mobiles than all the liquor in the world put together.

I can imagine all the young women sneering at this perfectly personal and logical theory with a monosyllable, 'Duh'. Now Duh is to women, what 'fuck' is to men. The Norwegian Nobel committee should seriously consider awarding a Nobel Prize for literature to those great men who invented these words. The world of literature would have been that much poorer without these great contributions. Half the world would go dyslexic. How many words can we toss up which can be used in every conceivable way – verb, adverb, adjective, gerund (now I am getting a little carried away).

Coming back to those lovely damsels, I do understand that the mobile to them is a life saving appendage more important than even a pacemaker and that they spend almost half of the day on it, but seriously, girls, have you considered the risks associated?

A couple of examples would suffice. A man is cheating on his wife. Pangs of guilt have destroyed his happiness. So he decides to give his wife a day to remember.

He comes home early with a bouquet of her favourite lilies and food ordered from her favourite Mainland China.

They have a great candle light dinner with Frank Sinatra and champagne for company.

Everything is picture perfect. The tense husband, afraid that nothing goes wrong, decides to have a shower before the last act. His bad luck, that when he is in the shower, his current flame, whose number he has so imaginatively saved as 'kitten' because she is so soft and cuddly, calls up. The wifey, who normally doesn't give a damn about his phone, has now been softened with all the pampering, lovingly picks up the phone. She feels it's her duty to help her 'stressed with business' husband.

Now, God, while creating Kitten wanted to be fair. So he reduced the size of her brain to that of a lima bean while showering her with bigger assets elsewhere. 'Hi Duhling. Hope that old bitch is not listening.' The kitten purrs seductively not for a moment thinking. The old bitch is not only listening but listening loud and clear. The Kitten can say good bye to her Tomcat forever. There would be just one mouse left.

Consider another situation. You are in the train and are an insomniac like me. With great difficulty you fall asleep. Suddenly two phones scream. One having the ring tone of 'Gayatri Mantra' which can waken up the gods in heaven and the another; 'My name is Sheila' which has woken Sheila sleeping in the third compartment from where we are. As for your jangling nerves, they are further jangled by the incessant chatter into the wee hours. You may as well say good bye to sleep.

On return to India, I had managed my life beautifully without a mobile or a watch or a pen for almost six months till I started this business.

I sneak into the toilet and downed two quick shots of Hundred Pipers.

Returning to my berth, I plug my iPod to block the annoying conversation the fellow passenger below was having on his mobile. I had no interest in his family problems.

Love can find many expressions. A certain Shahjehan built the Taj Mahal for his loved one. What is a train journey; however annoying.

As sleep engulfs me, I take another decision. I am not going to disclose the Heimlich maneuver involving Avantika. Love means not disclosing embarrassing incidents!

✦

I never knew that making a pizza is such a complicated affair. There were many equipment, most of them imported from the USA. There were two ovens, one makeline, one slap table, a walk-in freezer, a fryer and myriad other smaller things. My mind reeled at the thought of executing such a big project.

In contrast, software programming was like a walk in the park.

There was a long process before the pizza reached the customer's table. After so much effort, sometimes there were unsatisfied customers.

It was like group sex. Someone was always left dissatisfied.

Many times I had the temptation of running back. I had led a relatively easy life. Would it be possible for me to take such an arduous task? When I use 'I' it is, in fact, for both of us. But grammar or clear thinking were never my strong points. I was never an original thinker. Nachiket was. But I knew him well. Nachiket was also not very hard working.

But for the first time, I saw a hard glint in his eyes. I knew what it meant. We both didn't want to fail. There was no looking back now. We both had fallen in love with Manipal. For me there was that added attraction, Avantika. She had clearly moved from the periphery in my life to the centre of my existence. If I had to stay close to her, I had to live in Manipal. We had once again taken a right decision for the wrong reason.

Nachiket was right. There was no looking back. We then took one more decision. Till the project was executed, we would be off partying. We had to work twenty five hours a day.

We decided to spend more time with our consultant Ramachandran. He was a cranky old man and was constantly yelling. When he yelled, his sinews stood out. We prayed that they didn't burst before our project execution. But appearances can be deceptive. He had a great sense of humour. Unfortunately this man saved all of it for us. It was not funny then.

Our parents were very proud of us. They had never seen us so committed. They had never interfered in our life since we never went to them for money. His only grudge was that we were not serious about anything and flitted from one job to another and one project to another.

We were fortunate that they didn't know about our extra-curricular activities. My parents were a god-fearing couple. Mom prayed religiously and fasted at least twice a week. I don't know from where I got my wild streak. Perhaps I mutated somewhere on the way while growing up.

Once the ground work was done, we formally moved into our office. We had been working in it informally since my mother had not purified it with her pooja. She planned an elaborate pooja. There were four Brahmins chanting slokas and invoking the Gods. Nachiket and I were made to sit half naked in dhotis. We were trying to protect our modesty by preventing the dhoti from slipping down our loin and our eyes from the smoke coming out of the wooden twigs burning in the central havan. Avantika was trying hard not to laugh.

After enduring the torture for hours, we both agreed that we should relax our prohibitory order for a day. Avantika happily agreed. We all desperately needed a drink.

It had taken us twenty minutes to formulate disciplinary rules, within seventy-two hours we broke them.

My principal was right. We were anti-establishment!

✦

When God created women, he was, perhaps, smoking weed. Maybe I should be more specific, when he created Avantika. Avantika is absolutely unpredictable. She can handle the biggest jab sportingly but can sulk for a trivial matter the whole day.

We were at the pub. Avantika suggested that our music has to be really good. The best music system with woofers and a huge range covering everything from hip hop to rock to blues to house.

I feigned anger.

'Avantika. How dare you? We are a musical family. We have broken more records than the Jackson Five.' I waited for effect. 'The first album that I broke was a priceless Beatles when I was five, a good three years before Michael Jackson started sharing the lead with his brother Jermaine.'

Avantika giggled. She had given up on me. She predicted that our business would die even before it saw the light of day. I assured her that there was always a fifty percent chance of that happening. Nachiket said lets be realistic. Chances of failing were eighty percent. We both congratulated her on her cleverness and perspicacity.

I do not know what suddenly bugged her. Was it the drinks or our constant teasing?

Suddenly for no reason, she picked up her bag angrily. 'I really don't know what I saw in you.' Nachiket didn't realize that she was angry. He leered at her rubbing his crotch, 'Baby you haven't seen it yet.' In a flash, Avantika's purse flew in a rage. At that precise moment, I got up to go to the Men's. The purse hit me right on my cheek leaving me stunned. I felt a little wetness on my face. I still remember the purse very well. After this mishap I wasn't likely to forget it in a hurry.

As I rushed to the rest room to wash the wound, I tripped. Now I had a bleeding nose as well. I rushed to the basin to wash and looked at myself.

In my childhood, I was a very healthy boy. My visits to the hospital were far less than the other children of my age. While I could be proud of it, there was a downside to it. I was not used to seeing blood. The moment I saw blood it made me faint. My stomach just churned. Imagine my plight when I looked at my own face. It looked like someone had splashed a bottle of Maggi sauce on it. I simply passed out. When I woke up I found myself in a hospital with bandages on my head and plaster on my nose. I was later told that the hospital wouldn't let me in without a police complaint. My friends had to explain that there was no pub brawl. Pub brawls between sons of influential people's son is common and hence hospitals are wary of the backlash.

There was not much damage. The doctor laughed and said that probably I did more damage to myself by slipping and then passing out. Nachu, the smart ass that he was, quipped, that's not surprising. I was expecting Avantika to call and check on my health. It did not happen. I was dreaming of her coming with flowers and kissing me on my broken nose and apologizing. No such thing happened.

Sleeping in the hospital, all alone, I thought deeply. if we were not serious, I would lose out. I couldn't be a loser all my life.

My father and everyone knew that I had left the USA because I was tired of working for others. The truth was I was fired. I was caught watching porn in my office. No one knew about it. This was my last chance for redemption.

I quietly slipped out of the hospital. It was a large multi-specialty hospital. People were coming and going. My head was still bandaged. The doctor had assured me that it wasn't serious and the stitch marks would go away after a few days. I walked behind one man as if he was chaperoning me. The guard on duty was talking over the phone. He didn't even bother.

I wanted to meet Avantika desperately but once outside, I lost my confidence. What if she feel repulsed to see me like this?

I called up Nachiket. He was sitting in a pub. I told him that I wanted to meet him immediately. He was surprised.

'You don't need an appointment, buddy. Just haul your ass to Café F.'

I smiled. I was being stupid. Talking anything serious now was a waste of time.

I turned back towards the hospital. This time I was stopped by the security guard. He wouldn't allow me in without proper identification. I warned him that I would complain to the authorities that he was talking over the phone and didn't notice when I was leaving. He immediately let me go in but requested me not to leave the hospital again.

Life is indeed full of ironies. I was fine when I broke their rules but when I was trying to follow their rules, I was harassed.

✦

The time spent alone changed my attitude towards life. I was now working really hard. I spent most of my living hours in the office. There was an angry scar on my cheek which reminded me of my resolve. We had to work hard. If Nachiket didn't, I would work doubly harder. But we had to succeed.

In no time I was in total control. We had finalized the equipments, paid the advances and were now planning the store. All this in record time.

Each day I had to remind myself that I was a loser. I had to remove that tag.

✦

The Americans are like frogs in a well. Their life begins and ends in the radius of two thousand miles. Unsurprisingly the only Indians they know are the Red Indians. I was always mistaken for Spanish because of my black hair. Initially I tried to correct them. Then I gave up. I even started playing to them. To the liquor store girl in New Jersey, I was Juan. I complimented her on her general knowledge. She used to be delighted. 'It's the American education system. We are encouraged to learn even outside the class room.' I wholeheartedly agreed. She even claimed that her Spanish had improved because of me.

Then came a bug called Y2K which changed everything. Gone were the days of living in blissful inconspicuousness. Suddenly Indians were the toast of America. It happened because of a unique American propensity. The American brain and heart is where the dollar is. Y2K needed skilled software engineers in huge numbers. India became the perfect destination because in India every parent dreams that their son or daughter would either be a doctor or an engineer. Since medical college was expensive, the engineers proliferated resulting in not only plenty of skilled but also very cheap labor. America had hit a jackpot. When it became difficult to import that many engineers, some smart ass decided to export the project. Suddenly outsourcing came into the dictionary. India became the mecca of software companies.

The honeymoon didn't last long. The warts showed. It wasn't easy doing business. The common refrain was 'The Indians are very good in promising but very poor in delivering.' I fumed when I read it.

One evening, I was having a drink in Holiday Inn alone. I was sitting in a corner dunking croissant dipped in sambhar and washing it down with a glass of cold beer. I was missing Nachiket.

He had gone to Jammu with his mother to visit Vaishno Devi.

'Wow. This is what I call real fusion.' He bellowed. Like all Americans he was large and loud.

'I have a friend who has soup and beer together.' I didn't tell him that even this combination was the copyright of Nachiket.

'Buddy. You are talking to an American. We created the word weird. I have a friend who eats just one small cantaloupe in the whole day. He feels that it is enough to provide the necessary nutrients.' We immediately became friends.

I invited Gordon and handed him the menu. He mischievously said he would go with what I was having. After he settled with his beer, we got talking.

I asked him what brought him here. 'Business.' He was pleased to know that I had lived in Miami. 'What took you there?' 'Business' I said. He laughed loudly.

'Do you like it here?' He was quiet for a while collecting his thoughts. I knew he wanted to be careful so as not to offend me. He loved India he assured me. Loved the Indians too though they could be too friendly at times. I knew what he meant. The Indians could smother a stranger with their hospitality. The crowd and the heat bothered him. I smiled. It was clichéd.

Then he opened his box of woes. Four years and he had still not got a good partner. I was surprised. In Hyderabad, you throw a stone and it was sure to hit a software company. He shook his head. It was not the dearth of companies, it was the reliability factor. The delivery schedule. I was offended. Was he trying to say that the Indian software companies were inferior? He shook his head.

He lamented that in the last four years he had been unable to get one single reliable partner. Frustrated he started looking in other countries. He had no problem doing business with the Japanese whom he visited just twice; no problem with the Koreans too. But in spite of being in India for the last four years, he was struggling to find a good company. All the companies were quick to promise but seldom delivered. I shrugged him off by saying that maybe he met the wrong guys. He shook his head. I thought the spicy sambhar had shaken him.

But today when I am myself trying to do business in my own country, I too feel like shaking my head. Definitely it isn't because of the spicy sambhar.

The company importing the ovens from Middleby Marshall demanded an advance cheque for the entire amount. Additionally they demanded Rs. 40,000 since they would be airlifting it specially for us. Else the ovens would take at least three months to be delivered.

Their Sales Manager looked to be an honest man. He promised to deliver them to us in two weeks. He wasn't alone. It was the same story for all imports. The Italian tiles supplier also demanded an advance cheque. So did the artificial plants agent from Hong Kong.

Our consultant assured us that it was routine and for any imports, the vendors always demanded a total advance payment.

Soon I found out that two weeks meant maybe three or four or five weeks.

Once having paid the entire amount, we were now totally helpless.

Thank God men don't conceive. Else these men would have been pregnant all the time. Being an Indian, I had missed a very important trait of the Indians. They did not know how to say no.

When I asked the consultant what I should do, he advised me to try Pranayam.

Pranayam is an ancient breathing technique. What did it have to do with my equipment?

He smiled wickedly and said, 'Nothing. But it will help you relax your frayed nerves.'

I did not know that the old hag had a funny bone in him. Imagine two million bucks blocked. Only a psycho could smile.

I had a wicked urge to smother him, cut him off all the oxygen and when he went blue in his face, advise him to do Pranayam!

✦

Avantika refused to pick up my calls. I couldn't visit her house with the ugly bandage around my head. Nachiket was partying hard as usual and naturally had no time for me. On the other hand, free time was all I had. I suddenly felt very lonely.

It was certain that I had to do something meaningful to kill time before time killed me.

As a born and practicing Indian, three things came to my mind naturally – movies, cricket and politics. I ruled out all three.

Mrs. Sehgal visited me with her swamiji. She twitched at my sight. I was a hopeless case. Only the swami could help me. She looked at him to help me. Instead he looked at me dolefully with puppy eyes. I melted at the sight of those mournful eyes. I made a gesture promising that I would arrange his stuff soon. For Mrs. Sehgal's ears, he gave me a sermon which I listened like an obedient disciple. The swami apologized with his eyes. I forgave him. Occupational hazard. He lived on the largesse of rich cats like Mrs. Sehgal. He had to enact. But that small piece of oratory delighted Mrs. Sehgal no end. Her hard diamond eyes shone with the glint of success. She looked at me with a look that said she may have lost a hundred wars but she had finally won the battle. She had converted one more non-believer. How would she feel I wondered, if she knew that her great swami had succumbed to my charm.

Mother suggested praying. She wouldn't understand. My Gods were eclectic and were not confined by political boundaries. But I am sure she wouldn't certainly approve of most of them.

There was my biggest God, Lord Bacchus, the one who had always looked after me well. Then there was Hermes, the god of travel, with whose benevolence I had more to show on my passport than on my resume. The Indian Gods and Goddesses were not so benevolent. Alas, Goddess Saraswati and Goddess Laxmi, the goddesses of learning and wealth, never blessed me forgetting that even though my passport was renewed in Houston, my heart was that of a blue blooded Indian and they owed me some responsibility.

I racked my brain hard and then came to a conclusion. Travel was my anodyne for the moment

If it worked for so many years, there was no reason why it wouldn't work now.

I decided to visit Bhopal, the city of lakes. Bhopal and I had a very close connection. It was where my grandpa lived. From there, I decided, I would go for a day or two to Gwalior to meet some more relatives. When you have nothing much to do, it is a good idea to catch up with people who you would not otherwise have time to meet.

Grandpa was frail but had not lost any of his sharpness. Even today he wore a tie and wouldn't go out without a hat. He was delighted to see me. 'Good to see you sonny.' He hugged me hard. There was a twinkle in his eyes. 'There is everything that you would need. There is beer in the fridge, all your favourite movies stacked and Barbecue Nation has been intimated. Malhotra was joking that he could have the tandoor moved to our house.' Malhotra Uncle was the owner of Barbecue Nation, my favourite restaurant. I laughed. 'Grandpa. I don't have beer anymore.' He looked at me with concern. 'Is everything ok son?' 'Yes gram. Just need to be fit for my project.' I lied.

He laughed good naturedly. 'You are not working here. So it should be fine.' Again he paused for a while, 'Or else have scotch.' I agreed for beer. Just then the door bell rang. A boy was carrying snacks. Behind him, Uncle Malhotra was standing grinning from ear to ear. I ran and hugged him hard. He looked elegant as usual in his well ironed and starched pyjama kurta. He looked at me with pride. 'I heard that my son has now become an entrepreneur.' I blushed. 'Uncle. We have just started.' He accepted a scotch. After a couple of drinks, he excused himself. It was business time.

Grandpa and I were now alone.

'Movie?' again his eyes twinkled. I wanted to watch something that he would like. I was searching for some classics. He waved his hand. 'Have you watched Pulp Fiction?' I pretended as if I was dying to watch it. I hardly missed Quentin Tarantino's movies and had seen it probably a hundred times. But I had never enjoyed a movie so much. 'English motherfucker, do you speak it?' Samuel Jackson as the mob hit man was brilliant.

'Now if you will excuse me, I will go home and have a heart attack'. John Travolta was equally brilliant in his deadpan way. We almost fell on the floor laughing. Grandpa was sitting on his favourite rocking chair and I was sitting on the floor besides him. I didn't want the movie or the evening to end. It was simply magical. Perhaps we would have enjoyed even a mediocre movie because the movie was just an excuse to enjoy each other's company.

Long after the movie was over, we sat there sharing the silence. When the spoken words are exhausted, silence is the only language of communication.

He was tousling my hair. 'Sonny, don't take life too seriously. You seem to be under some sort of stress?'

My heart felt heavy. Nothing was going right. I hadn't seen Avantika for a week. All that frustration melted in the warmth of his affection. I wanted to scream and tell him about how I felt. But I just sat there scratching the floor with my thumb. Grandpa didn't believe in interfering. He didn't broach any further.

I rose and walked to the window. There was a large lake behind the house. The water was still. The street lights reflected in the water. Malhotra Uncle came back with a retinue of waiters bringing trays and trays of delicious dinner. His arrival made the atmosphere a bit lighter. Later, I gently led Gram to his bedroom and helped him sleep. When I heard his gentle snoring, I quietly closed the door. But sleep eluded me. I picked up my jacket and decided to go out for a walk.

There was nip in the air. My heart felt heavy. I knew perhaps it would be one of the last times I would be seeing grandpa. As I walked, my mind raced back taking me down memory lane. Memories came, first in a rush and then gradually settled. I felt like I was watching a movie.

I was a little boy riding on Grandpa's shoulders, mother embarrassed and gently chiding him that people were watching and Grandpa saying the prince shall not walk on the road and I giggling with happiness. The Annual Day where I am acting in my first play. It is a very short part. I had barely to utter three sentences. But grandpa as proud as if I was the hero of the play. Grandma bringing piping hot jalebi's in the wintery morning and tickling me to wake up but I refusing to get out of the warm and comfortable bed. Finally we both eating on the bed much to our amusement and mother's anger.

Grandma's funeral. Grandpa sitting stony faced, not betraying any emotions. Suddenly the movie stopped.

I found myself sitting on the kerb just like him, stony faced, not betraying any emotions.

Sometimes when grief becomes unbearable, the tears dry up even before they reach the eyes. The same tears which were eager to roll out following grandpa's gentle touch, were now obstinate and refused to come out even after aggressive prodding.

I screamed out in frustration. A mangy dog was lying on the other side of the road. He was startled but again went back to sleep. He was not a street dog for nothing.

It takes one insomniac to understand the pain of another one. I was looking for some compassion. All I could find was this dog. Vengefully, I picked up a stone and hurled it at him. The dog gave a long yelp and again settled down to sleep. I gave up. Nothing could be done. We both were incorrigible. He a 'hypersomniac' and me an insomniac.

My mind in turmoil, sleep eluded me. I went back home and made some hot cocoa then curled on the sofa with old photo albums found in Grandpa's library. It was fun seeing the sepia tinted photographs of grandpa and grandma and dad as a kid.

I do not know when I fell asleep. But I slept like a baby. I knew I had grown up when I woke up on the same sofa where I fell asleep. If I were a baby I would have woken in my bed no matter where I fell asleep. Gram always picked me up and took me to bed.

I heard the gentle footsteps of Gram in the room. 'Morning. Gram.' He chuckled. 'Have you seen the time?' I couldn't believe it. It was 11.30 am. I asked him if he had his breakfast. He just smiled. Ashamed I told him to give me a few minutes and I would be at the table.

Later we decided to go and explore the city. Bhopal, though the capital of Madhya Pradesh, is still an overgrown village. It is a curious blend of old world and the modern. One can see brand new shopping malls jostling space with traditional shops. Old tailors bending over their sewing machines or traditional barbers shaving under a tree with old fashioned razors. The pungent local attar competed spiritedly with expensive brands of imported perfumes in the shops on Hamidia Road. The *ittar* is the extract of fragrant oils from flowers. Perfumes have killed the business of *ittars* which is now limited to Poojas, but the tradition is still alive in Bhopal. Elderly Muslim men still preferred it over perfumes. These *ittars* are purchased from the narrow lanes of Dariba Kalan in Old Delhi. Slowly, yet surely, the old traditions are dying elsewhere but not in this spirited city.

It was hard to believe that this city had seen the worst industrial disaster in 1984 when a Union Carbide plant leaked about thirty-two tonnes of toxic gases killing thousands of men and rendering hundreds sick. After two decades the people still have to receive compensation. But Indians have a great buoyancy. This city refuses to show any scars of that horrible event.

We lunched at the old Jehanuma Palace, Gram's favourite. As we sat in the elegant ambience of Shahnama, the multi-cuisine restaurant, sipping red wine and tearing into the delectable kebabs, Grandpa asked me what was my plan. I told him I wanted to spend a day in Gwalior before going back.

He was about to say something but then decided to remain silent. I asked him something which I had been longing to ask, 'Grandpa. Why don't you come with me? We can live together.' He had a faraway look in his eyes. 'Memories son. I spent the best time of my life here with your grandmother. Even today I feel her spirit in the house. I feel she may walk into the room any moment with a cup of tea in her hand.' Then he suddenly smiled and winked, 'If she really did, it would scare the daylight's out of me though.' That was grandpa. He could successfully camouflage his sorrow with his mischievous smile.

I had that urge to bear hug him and not let him go. But being a boy has its drawbacks. Any physical show of affection is considered lame. If I were a girl, I could have slobbered him and no one would even have noticed.

So I just sat there and looked dotingly at my best friend.

Tomorrow I shall be leaving for Gwalior.

Mother is a strong believer in astrology. She believes that nothing moved without the permission of the stars in the constellation. Maybe there was some truth in it. I found myself at the Raja Bhoj Airport the next day as planned. Only I had to take a different flight.

I had received two calls that night. One from the consultant urgently asking me to report to Hyderabad. The ovens had finally landed in Mumbai and my signature was required on some documents. That could still have waited. It was the second call which was defining. It came from a new number. Normally I am wary of picking up a new call. Lucky I did. It was from a girl called Avantika!!!

✦ ✦ ✦

V

I pity those who fall in love.
I did not fall.
Like a feather,
I gently glided into it.

On landing, I drove straight to the consultant's office. The good news was that the ovens had landed. The bad news was that we needed some documents from the Government. Till then I had only heard of the harrowing tales one encountered in government offices. I was to now see it first hand. Ramchandran told me that he was being paid for arranging all these. But I wanted to teach that bastard a lesson. I wanted to show him that I could manage even without his help. I wish I hadn't.

In the USA, you could form a new company by opening a current account in the bank and start an office in a matter of days. The documents requirement was minimum and so was the bureaucracy. Bribing was something unheard of. In India, it was the opposite.

Visiting the government office was a cruel reminder of how little I knew about my own country. The Indian Government was a basket case. It had no control over any Department. I learnt that each Minister decided on a target bribe for his department. It was the department's responsibility to send the Minister his bribe per month. Once the lion got his share, he left the carcass to the other animals. Then it was the department's talent of how much money they made. Bribes were not optional. Departments believed in the traffic slogan, 'Speed Kills.' You couldn't fast track anything. But they were not just crooks, they were smart crooks and knew how to cover themselves. They delayed with massive paper work. There was no accountability. The documents were drafted in such a manner that one couldn't sue the Government for anything. Every document, be it of any department, needed to be given in triplicate, which meant that any submission to any department wouldn't be less than one hundred pages. It entailed a number of affidavits and undertakings. One had to furnish proof of everything under the sun. To make matters worse, there was nothing like an integrated office. If you had to deal with two desks in the same office, you had to submit a separate set of documents to each one of them. The offices seemed to crumble under the weight of these papers. There was no place to even store them. Go to any government office and you will see tonnes of files lying abandoned like orphans on the floor. Once submitted, the files would be carelessly thrown on a mountain of files which were already lunch to termites. One could occasionally see fat rats scurrying under those files. I promised myself that I wouldn't touch any of the files that returned from any department. It was a miracle that government employees never fall sick. Perhaps even the rodents know better.

Even though bribe was rampant, you needed the help of a tout. If you needed anything from a ration card to a driving license or a trade license to a sales tax registration, you couldn't move without a tout.

These guys were to the department what a pimp was to a prostitute.

I remembered that when I had opened a company in the US, all they asked for was my social security number. It took less than an hour.

The consultant, to borrow a chat word, was ROFL. He enjoyed my discomfiture. He then took over from me. I received the documents in three days. The pimp had managed.

I was planning in my mind ways of killing him and passing it off as an accident. But secretly I knew I needed him. I couldn't do anything without him.

I had to be patient. Soon I wouldn't need this sadist. Till then I had to keep my temper in check. You don't snatch defeat from the jaws of victory.

Better to act dumb and win rather than look smart and lose.

✦

I met Avantika in Aalankrita, a very romantic four star resort near Hyderabad. The resort was a paradise for romance. Far from the city, amid lush green grass, exotic flora and fauna and dense foliage, it provided every comfort. It had elegant rooms for staying, various delightfully named restaurants serving delicious multi-cuisine food, a well stocked bar, a swimming pool, gaming zone and acres and acres of green space.

Avantika wore a flowing lavender coloured dress. Her hair was tied in a pony tail making her look very young. She was wearing minimum makeup. My heart was beating fast. She looked so achingly beautiful.

She smiled broadly when she saw me. I hugged her hard knowing how much I had missed her.

We decided to eat in Atiroopa, an elegant restaurant done in a very ethnic style. The walls were done up in red bricks and there were exquisite wooden carvings on pillars and at the entrance. The large doors too were intricately carved with multi-coloured glasses inside. The tables and chairs were heavy and made of teak wood. The place was bathed in golden yellow giving it a very romantic feel. There was a large swing just outside. For the unadventurous, there were sofas everywhere with thick red rugs below. The colourful cushions and the oriental upholstery gave it a palace-like look. The usher was a tall turbaned man who had thick big moustaches and bent forward as he opened the door and made you feel like royalty when you entered. It oozed class.

'Hmm. Looks like the scar has healed.' She joked even before we settled down. I laughed easily. This was one girl who I could laugh with.

'Yeah. If you want them to remain, hit me harder next time.'

She giggled. 'You idiot. I wasn't even hitting you. I was hitting Nachiket' I looked at the bag. The purple leather bag looked beautiful except that the Rhinestone broach was missing exposing the naked screw. Now I knew the reason for the scar. I guessed that it must have been made in China. For my safety, I promised to buy her an expensive bag for her next birthday. Something which could hold the broach more strongly. She laughed. 'No silly. This purse was bought in Jaipur'.

'Ok. But why didn't you come to see me in the hospital.'

'I didn't even know you are in hospital.' She giggled again. What was she, a giggle machine!

'I didn't know you were such a sissy.' I ignored the jab.

'You could have called me.'

'You idiot, I lost my phone.'

'But you could have called Nachu.'

'Once again. You idiot I had lost my phone.'

'You could have asked Mr. Gupta.'

'You idiot he is my father.' That made sense. He still didn't know about our relationship.

Suddenly she asked, 'But then why didn't you come to meet me?'

I was enjoying it now. It was my chance to get even. I mimicked her.

'You idiot. I was in hospital.' The giggling, forgotten for some moments, started again.

Gently she touched that almost invisible scar with her finger and then kissed me on the scar. I couldn't hold back. I grabbed her by her shoulder and kissed her hard on her lips crushing them with my urgency. It was a very aggressive kiss. It contained all my frustrations and loneliness. She didn't resist and fell limply in my arms. How could I think that she could have been angry with me for a non-issue.

Status quo restored, I suddenly wanted to move back to my good old days of drinking. A leopard cannot change its spots. We ordered Carlsberg. I am sure her father would have choked on his food once again if he knew that his daughter was a champion beer guzzler or that she had a greater love for the fauna than the flora and that was not in the biology class.

She was happily enjoying the succulent meat marinated in fiery spices and roasted in the Indian Tandoor with the cool beer. I was simply watching her. I needed nothing else.

Happiness is the celebration of love. There is no definition for happiness. We were happy in our corner of the world. We sat in that corner of our paradise till the sun, who was hitherto not visible to us, decided that enough was enough and it was time to go home without even saying good bye.

We reached home late. It was a dark night. The only stars were in our eyes. For the first time in my life I realized the difference between love and sex. I had to agree that romance was the champagne of all emotions. I could live my whole life on love alone without so much as even touching Avantika.

✦

A bawdy Punjabi song was playing on the cheap tape recorder. 'It is Sawan, the month of showers. The flowers are blooming and romance is in the air'. The girl is trying to woo her boyfriend with her charm. Satnam Singh smiled and winked at Chavanni. He asked him if he was missing his girl friend. Chavanni was his fifteen year old cleaner. This was not his real name. Chavanni is a quarter of a rupee which is rarely used these days. It is a derogatory term to describe a minor. He blushed. Satnam Singh laughed loudly.

They were carrying our oven from Mumbai to Bengaluru. It would be unloaded into a warehouse in Bengaluru first from where it would be loaded into another lorry and sent to Manipal. This was necessary as we wanted it to be billed from Bengaluru and not Mumbai. If they billed us from Mumbai, we would get no VAT refund. We would then pay a 2% central sales tax against what they called a C Form.

Chavanni was holding their lunch lovingly packed by Satnam's wife, Bebo. She was a Jat woman who believed in feeding her husband well. Lunch was a typical Punjabi fare consisting of rotis made of wheat, mango pickle, a chunk of home made butter and a curry made of fried potatoes and cauliflower. She handed the carrier along with a large bottle of lassi – thick butter milk – to Chavanni.

After three hours, they reached a hilly terrain. The road was winding and narrow. The lorry was wheezing as it slowly circled the rocky hill.

He affectionately asked the boy if he was hungry. The boy shook his head. He promised the boy that once they reached the plain, they will take a break to eat.

There were blind curves. Satnam was an expert driver and was used to driving on these roads. He was negotiating each curve carefully. He knew that one small mistake and they would be in the bottomless pit.

There was traffic from the other side too which was making driving more difficult. The bawdy song was long forgotten as Satnam now concentrated hard.

Suddenly a Toyota carrying a family lost its control from the other end. Satnam cursed in chaste Punjabi as he tried to steer clear of the oncoming projectile. But there was not enough room. The truck lost control and turned turtle. All one could hear were the screams of Chavanni and the choicest abuses of Satnam as the lorry went into the bottomless pit.

I woke up with a scream. It was a scary nightmare. I found myself on the floor all jittery and sweating. My fall was buffered by the blanket. I escaped any injury. But my mind was elsewhere.

It was a wake up call. We had tried to save money on insurance. That was foolish. If such an accident happened, we would loose millions.

I decided that the first thing I would do was call up the insurance agent tomorrow. Not only the oven, I decided that we shall take the insurance for all the equipments. It was hard to sleep after this terrible nightmare.

I got up and made myself some strong coffee. We were rank amateurs. We had to hire a professional.

I called Nachiket to discuss appointing a Project Manager. As expected, the call went unanswered. I smiled. He could not be woken up even if there was an earthquake.

I opened my laptop and added this task to the 'To Do' list. Habits, specially good ones, take time. Slowly I was getting to do things systematically.

After this nightmare, I decided to take no chances and visit Bengaluru and see the status of the equipments being manufactured. I sent emails to all the manufacturers asking them for a suitable date for inspection.

To my surprise I got an immediate reply from one supplier. He was Krishnaiah, the makeline manufacturer.

Immediately I went on chat and asked him what was he doing at such an ungodly hour. He replied that they had an important consignment to be dispatched and hence the night out. I was impressed. He seemed a thorough professional.

I then enquired if he knew anyone who could look after my project. Yes, there was one experienced guy who had just returned from Sharjah and was looking for a project. His name was Ganesh. He was an ex-army man. Krishnaiah rated him highly. I promised to meet him when I was in Bengaluru.

I felt better now. But still sleep was elusive. Masturbation always had a soporific effect. But not tonight. My mind was too agitated. I opened my briefcase and opened the file sent by Correa. It had detailed bar charts and drawings of each thing. Ramchandran had sent a detailed plan of the kitchen with each equipment's position and the location of basins. Based on them, Correa had visited the site and seen the location of the water pipes and prepared the plumbing designs. Clearly our investment had not gone waste. I felt a new respect for Ramchandran. He may be a social outcaste but the guy sure knew his job. He somehow didn't like me and mocked at my professional knowledge but with Correa he was very professional.

I became so involved in reading the drawings that I didn't even realize when it was morning. A ray of sunshine found its way through the blinds.

My eyes were red. But deep within there was a turmoil. We had to be more serious. I had to talk to Nachiket about this someday. Each and every boy has to grow up into a man one day. That is nature's scheme of things. It is not linked to one's biological age. Some take the stairs some take the elevator. But time doesn't stop for anyone. Each one of us has to grow up either on our own or with someone's help, some do it easily some the hard way.

When I called my father to discuss about the insurance, I found out that we were insured after all. Dad had already done that for us. I suddenly realized how naïve we had been. We thought that our parents had just signed up as guarantors.

They were there every step. I was sure if the situation arose, they would jump in and take control.

Luckily that situation didn't arise.

Once I resumed drinking, Nachu and I were once again on the same plane.

We decided that I would go to Manipal first and find a place to live and then Nachu would join me. We decided to split the work. Since I was going earlier, I would be in charge of the construction. I was carrying all the structural drawings. Correa had painstakingly prepared them. He promised to visit me once the work began. Nachiket would be in charge of the interiors.

He had to order the sofas, the chairs, the counter and the other interiors whereas I had to hunt for a good plumber, electrician and a civil contractor. We had decided to break one wall and have a large wall to ceiling window from one end to the other end. Also we had planned to have Italian tiles for the counter. They were not ordinary tiles and we needed specially skilled guys to fix them. Similarly we had opted for texture painting. I had to look for those experts as well. There was formidable work involved.

✦

There are times when you want to believe in God.

As I walked out of my cab, a drop of water fell on my head. I looked up excitedly. It must be the monsoon. Just then a bird dropping bombarded me in my eye. I thanked God that cows couldn't fly.

The watchman saw me and didn't show any expression that would mean that he was happy to see me back.

I wasn't expecting anyone and found no one in the apartment. So I deposited my belongings and walked out.

It was time now to leave this apartment and find a place of my own. It wasn't easy to find an apartment in Manipal. There were over thirty-five thousand rich students. Only a small percentage could be accommodated in the hostel. Rest lived in apartments.

Availability was a bigger issue. I braced myself for a long search.

But inspiration is like the Manipal rains. It comes unannounced.

Before venturing out on a house search, I decided to drop by at my landlord. His secretary asked me to wait outside as the landlord was busy over the phone. I could hear agitated voices inside. Shortly afterward, I saw a one young boy storming out angrily.

I would be blind if I didn't notice that he was a junkie. As soon as he spotted me, he was spewing invectives on my hapless landlord. I asked him what happened. It turned out that at 3 am. some of his other junky friends (I am guessing that they are junkies too) wanted to meet this boy. The watchman refused to let them in as guests were not allowed after 11 p.m. The venerable friends were not used to taking no for an answer. They bashed up the poor man. The owner reported the matter to the boy's father in Orlando and even went a step further and informed him that his son was a junkie. The boy warned me to be careful of this evil man and not take his apartment on lease. I wholeheartedly agreed without bothering to tell him that I had more than an apartment tied with him. We signed the lease-deed soon enough. Officially we now had our own home in Manipal.

✦

It took me a week's time to appoint the various contractors. I also visited Bengaluru and visited the factories and inspected. The makeline, the cut table, ducting and chutes were going as per the schedule. There was some delay in the walk-in but even that was not alarming. I sent a formal appointment letter to Ganesh.

Satisfied, I was now returning by the afternoon flight to Manipal. I was getting a feel of it now. I had to now concentrate on the recruitments and send the staff for training. They would work for at least forty-five days in an existing Pizza joint to gain practical experience.

✦

The recruitments were a disaster. The ads in the newspaper did not elicit a single response. I visited every pub and restaurant in town. Not a single guy was interested. Finally, tired, depressed and dejected I did what I was good at. I went to a bar and got drunk. But this surely was not the solution. I had to still find the staff. But how? I imagined myself if I were Mr. Gupta. What would he have done? Nothing emerged. I had got to think hard tomorrow.

✦

Ketan, a bright looking young man, came to meet me. He had been sent by our Bank Manager. He lacked experience but seemed ambitious and not short in drive. Best part was that he had some experience in working in a pizzeria. He was asking for more salary than my budget allowed but I decided that I had to compromise somewhere. I give him an option. I asked him to show his talent in recruiting staff. The guy was pure dynamite!

In less than forty-eight hours, we had more than twenty-five applicants. When I looked at the resumes, I was surprised to see the names of many of them who had rejected me when I had approached them. Ketan told me that he spoke Tulu and that is where the difference lay. They considered him as one of them and hence trusted him. I swallowed my pride and began to interview the applicants.

But my ego was bruised. I tried hard to convince myself that I was smarter than Ketan. After all I had the smartness to employ him in the first place. But I was unable to convince myself.

I was a good-for-nothing guy. Nachiket didn't even try and cheer me up.

✦

I have thrown a party for the newly appointed staff. Nachiket approved of it. But Shenoy warned us. "This is not a software company. The staff is uneducated. Don't give them too much leeway or they will take undue advantage." I think he has a point. There are a lot of things that I still have to learn. I decide to make it a simple party minus the drinks. I distributed their appointment letters and made announcement about their training in Bengaluru. There is a commotion. They have many questions. I and Ketan, patiently answer. Most of them have never left Manipal and hence are naturally scared. I joke with them and tell them that there are human beings in Bengaluru and none of them bite. The staff laughs nervously. I tell them that there are nice cinema halls. They can watch cricket match.

They can visit shopping malls and ogle at sexy girls. They titter shyly. I tell Ketan to open files for each of them. Take their details including their mobile numbers and the contact person in case of emergency.

Satisfied that one chapter is closed, I have to now concentrate on the interior design and the engineering. Secretly I pray for Ganesh to arrive. But till he comes at least we can make a beginning. Ramchandran is arriving tomorrow with Correa. I pray harder for Ganesh. Can't stand this oaf.

✦

Ramchandran has called for a meeting of all the main suppliers. Correa, fortunately has no ego and plays second fiddle. He is terse but quite efficient. Everyone is explained his scope of work and handed a bar chart with the time schedule. I am impressed. Just when I feel I must praise him, he snatches the drawings from my hand and naughtily says, 'These are drawings son. They may look pretty but you need training to understand them.' I feel like pushing him into the jungle. No one would know. Hopefully some wild animal would make a meal of him.

But would even an animal eat this obnoxious man?

Correa is unflappable. As long as he is paid, he doesn't care.

✦

Things have started to move. It is an orgy involving men and their formidable tools. Some of these tools are power driven. Nachu laughs. Our brains are really in our groin.

✦

The place has turned into a bedlam of noise, dust and sweat. Wooden shavings are flying with abandon, dancing to the rhythmic music of the planer and the regular beats of the hammers. The masons are busy with bricks and cement laying the foundation of a crazy dream. The electricians are pouring over complex drawings instructing their assistants to dig holes in the walls for laying cables that would provide power to the equipment.

I just sit there mesmerized, watching them at work. They are not artisans but artists giving bones and muscles to our fantasy.

I was watching them intently at work. Suddenly I fainted.

I had not realized it but the temperature was soaring. I had never been out in the sun for so long. The doctor was a young man and with an overflowing sense of humor.

'So what's your problem?' I was already feeling better.

'I see ghosts.' I whispered, trying to imitate Haley Osment.

'Careful. She is my wife and she has ears.' He whispered. I got up from the bed laughing.

'How are you feeling now?'

'Feeling flattened like a pita bread.'

'Hmm. So let's put some stuffing into it.' He had ordered for a drip despite my protestations. He was gentle but firm. The glucose won't do any harm, he assured.

I tried to wriggle out of the situation. 'Doc, this is the time for beer, not sugar.'

He looked at his watch and promised that he would release me in an hour.

'In good time for a drink' he laughed. I resigned myself to fate.

I warned him that I would be eating an apple everyday. He laughed and said, 'There goes my consultancy fees in future.'

I dozed off while watching the News, fitfully dreaming that I was tied to the chair by pastas and a dimpled boy approaching with a ladle of pasta sauce menacingly and dunking me in it with some solid support from his mother.

At one point he comes and violently shakes me. I wake up all sweaty. Nachiket has come to pick me up. He had gone to the sofa maker to finalize the sofas. All through the ride he keeps ribbing me about being sissy. I have run out of excuses.

Avantika and her gang came in the evening to meet the 'patient'. I had no other option but to surrender to their ragging. I fish out a bottle of Hundred Piper and a half bottle of gin and lime cordial. But the guys wouldn't have any of it.

'You have come back from the dead. We must have a bigger party.' Nachu was enjoying my embarrassment. After a long discussion, it was decided that we would go to Om Beach.

'Om Beach! Are you guys crazy? Its already seven in the evening.'

They all laughed. God these guys were weird. It was decided that we shall stay in a hotel overnight and then spend the whole of next day at the beach.

I protested. We had just begun work. 'Come on Tejas. Even Jesus sleeps on Sundays.' 'Hey Jesus was not starting a pizzeria.' But they would have none of it.

Immediately a Toyota was summoned. We already had coolers which were filled with ice and beers. Two guys went for the snacks. It was a four hour's journey.

I tried one last time. 'It is a weekend. The hotels may be full.'

But I knew better. Once they decided, nothing could deter them. Besides even I knew. There were many resorts nearby. So we would definitely get some place to sleep overnight. These guys were truly Bohemians. It wouldn't worry them much to sleep anywhere.

By the time we started, it was already eight. It became very loud and clear to me. I had to do two things. One, never to faint again. Two, if I had to complete the project in time, I had to limit my socializing. That meant I would have to avoid Avantika's friends. Initially I thought that Avantika would be offended. But she chided me instead for not doing it sooner.

Avantika had given a new meaning to my life. It was like I had turned over a new leaf.

Everything was on a roll. Nachiket was doing a fantastic job. We had liked the design of the sofa and approved it immediately. Our interior was going well. The granite cutters were busy cutting granite for the floor border, the counter and the tables. The false ceiling team were busy erecting the grid work of metal channels in the shape of an upside down 'T'. It would be closed only after the ducting and wiring was over in the plenum space. The artificial plants would be arriving from Hong Kong in a week's time.

Nachu was pleased with all the accolades coming his way. He thought it meant a blanket visa to indulge in all kind of amorous activities.

Suddenly we received a bad news. Nachiket's dad had slipped from the stairs and broke his hip bone and was in the hospital. Although he was taking it bravely and strictly instructed Nachiket not to visit him as time was precious now, we thought it fit to go only for a day.

Avantika also wanted to come but had some important submissions. We assured her that we would return in a few days time.

Ram Bharose assured us that he would manage the show. We gave him some cheques so that the project didn't starve for funds in our absence. We both laughed after he left. We didn't have any illusions. For us, this project was beyond our abilities and were it not for the assuring presence of Ram Bharose, we would have been all lost. He was managing the show even in our presence. We were missing Ganesh badly.

Nachiket suggested that we could stop by at Bengaluru and see the progress of our equipment and take the evening flight instead. I was delighted. Nachiket was totally focused now. Besides we loved the biryani in Majestic.

Bengaluru was once upon a time a veritable paradise. It had a multi-dimensional facet. On the one hand it was known as the pensioner's paradise, on the other hand it was the hub of a technological revolution. The old and new lived in perfect harmony. There was something for everyone. The city had a cool climate. The roads were clean and lined with tall magnificent trees which not only increased its aesthetics but also helped in keeping the streets cool during the summer. Its cool climate attracted birds of all kinds. Alas, it had to end one day. Along with the sobriquet 'Silicon Valley of India' came the trappings of money. It ruthlessly crushed the spirit of Bengaluru. Software ushered in a new middle class who could now afford a more lavish lifestyle. So now there were more cars on the streets. There was more money in the pocket. It made Bengaluru the pub capital of India. But it also brought along with it pollution, traffic congestion and an alarmingly high cost of living. I shudder every time I come to

Bengaluru not knowing how much time it will take for me to reach the city from the airport.

Fortunately the traffic wasn't that bad. We finished our inspection and were pleased with the progress. The equipments were almost ready to be shipped.

Our work done, we went to Nandini on our way we walked into one of the bars. Nandini unfortunately didn't have a bar. We would have preferred to eat the biryani with beer. But rules were rules. Just the thought of the spicy, aromatic biryani with tender succulent chunks of meat made our mouth water.

We rushed to the restaurant and as expected had to wait our turn. Nachiket was checking his watch. But I was in no mood to leave without eating.

As we dug into the delicately cooked tender meat pieces, inhaling the aroma, we thought it was worth the wait. Hyderabad, our home town, was supposed to be the cradle of this dish. But this restaurant could give it a run for its money. We promised ourselves that we would try the biryani in Hyderabad and compare. Suddenly we felt nostalgic. Manipal could fare in other things but not in food.

The food was bland as compared to the spicy and mouth watering Andhra cuisine. Hyderabad was a gourmet's delight. The list of delicacies belonging to Hyderabad was long. We tested our knowledge to see how many of them we knew.

We didn't even realize that we had long left the city and boarded the flight to Hyderabad. Still the list was not even half-over. We talked about the perennial favourites – Biryanis and the very rich and sweet *Khubani ka meetha* made from apricot, the calorie rich *Double ka meetha* and the seasonal *Haleem* available only during the month of Ramzaan. It was my favourite. Made from wheat, barley, lentils, and ground meat along with heavenly spices, this is slow cooked on a earthen hearth for seven to eight hours to get a paste-like consistency. This was a staple food during Ramzaan. During Ramzaan, the Muslims do not drink water or eat anything the whole day. Eating *Haleem* ensured that they did not feel hungry or thirsty the whole day. We talked about *Nihari*, the delicious soup made from goat's tongue. We tried naming some vegetarian specialilies *Baghar baingan*, stuffed aubergines, *Mirchi ka saalan* – spicy curry made of green chillies we laughed. 'Mirchi Bhajji' Nachu piped. We could name only three.

We congratulated each other on knowing at least thirty of them. We were both sure that we must have certainly missed at least ten more.

Shortly after, the plane landed at the Rajiv Gandhi Airport. All this talk of food had made us very hungry. We rushed to have a sandwich in Subway.

'It has low calories.' I grinned.

But now it was time to sober down. Uncle was admitted in hospital and we were not sure how serious he was till we saw him. Sometimes silence is the perfect medicine for a troubled mind. I decided to leave Nachu alone as we drove to the hospital.

As soon as we reached the hospital, I squeezed Nachu's hands. 'Don't worry, everything will be alright. Be brave.' With that I rushed to the rest room and puked. Hospitals did that to me. I came out of the rest room white faced and wobbly. I felt empathy for the old man. But when we went inside, he looked fit. Unlike me, he had taken the visit very bravely. Some people are made of sterner stuff!

Flirting with the nurses and joking with the doctors, he seemed to have become their favourite patient.

'He will live long enough to bury us both.' I whispered. This time Nachu had a genuine smile on his lips.

Uncle looked frail. It was a relief to see him recuperating well. He was pleased to see us though he feigned anger that we had neglected our work and come to see him. We showed him the progress on Nachu's iPad. My father was also there. They both looked pleased as punch. We could not stay long as he was under sedation most of the time to ease the pain and moreover, the visiting hours were over.

We were standing in the porch of the magnificent hospital when Dad came from behind. 'So guys what is your plan for the evening? You can take my car if you like. I will go in an auto.' Nachu thanked him and said that we would rather pick up his bike. Dad offered to drive us till Nachu's house. He was genuinely happy with what we were doing. I could feel it in his voice. He was never that emotional.

Nachiket believed that the motorcycles were meant to fly. He decided to take a short cut. We were heading for the Mecca of good food, the Charminar, meant only for hardcore foodies. Not even a brush of sophistication has reached it. I remember one of my ex girlfriend had wrinkled her powdered nose and described it as 'tacky'. She dumped me the next day itself. We changed ourselves from the next day. No girls ever came with us to this place again.

Soon we were tearing into *Pathar ke gosht* – succulent chunks of meat cooked on stone – and large pieces of bread, dunking them into the delectable *Nihari*.

Between mouthfuls, Nachiket ordered *Dum biryani* with the spicy *Mirchi ka saalan* and yoghurt. It was inevitable that we finish our dinner with a typical Hyderabadi dessert. We argued hotly whether to go for *Khubani ka meetha* or *Double ka meetha*. Unable to come to a conclusion, we ordered for both. It turned out it wasn't a very wise thing to do. When we were returning, Nachiket was dozing off while driving. Finally I had to take up the driving with Nachiket leaning over me all asleep.

The return trip to Manipal was uneventful. We both were in a hurry to return to work. I marveled at how much we had changed. Now the only thing that mattered was work. Our young naive idealistic mind believed that we were in utopia and that only hard work and dedication counted. Alas, we had forgotten that there was a worm in the apple. That worm was *babudom*, the corrupt bureaucracy. There was a survey which had mentioned that India was the second most corrupt country in the world. Nachu wryly commented that we were the most corrupt country but our government bribed them to show us as second.

✦ ✦ ✦

VI

Pythons and worms spoil the party

One day a representative from the labour department came and asked to see our labour license. We just blinked. No one had told us about it. He threatened to bring down the shutters if we couldn't produce it. We were shocked. Our project was in the most critical stage and we couldn't disturb the momentum. I looked at Ram Bharose. He shrugged his shoulder in resignation. He was an artisan. He could create anything out of wood. But men, no, he had no experience with them.

I then remembered of Shenoy. He would be the best person to deal with this slime ball. Shenoy told me not to worry. The moment the labor officer saw Shenoy, his expressions changed. They met like two long lost friends. After enquiring about each other's families, Shenoy turned to Ram Bharose and asked if they had ordered tea. He gave him a hundred bucks and asked him to send someone for tea and set dosas.

Then he ushered the officer to his room. After twenty minutes both of them walked out hand in hand. Mr. Shenoy signaled me to meet him in a corner. He explained that it was routine. No one ever closed anything in India. If they close your business how would they make money. He told me to pay him ten thousand. I asked Shenoy if this was official. Shenoy laughed. Official payments have to be made by cheque. This was bribe. I looked at that slime ball. He suddenly got busy taking out a very old and musty notebook with yellowing pages. Then slowly he took out a carbon paper. He tore the carbon into two and inserted the two papers making a certificate in triplicate. I hated to think of accepting that certificate. The paper was already old and musty.

Meanwhile I went to an ATM and withdrew the money. When I came back I noticed a small crowd gathered by the side of the road. Two monkeys were dancing under the instructions of their master. I can swear that one of the monkeys looked like the government officer.

✦

When the Municipal Officer came for the trade license, we did not call Shenoy this time. Now we knew the ropes.

I was confident that now nothing could stop our work. Perhaps I had underestimated. There was more to life than Government officers.

There was nothing in the morning that portended any catastrophe. It was a normal morning with ominous black clouds, a ear shattering lightning and power outage. All this was normal in Manipal. It would be wrong to say that the monsoon had arrived. The truth was that the monsoon had never left.

We had planned to purchase an auto generator switch for the generator. But it was expensive. So we were currently managing with manual switch. This meant that the security guard had to go and switch on the generator whenever there was a power failure.

Our security guard was an old Nepali man named Bahadur. We had hired him a month back but had immediately rued our decision. He was old and couldn't see properly. He slept during night duties and that was a major cause of worry. If he didn't wake up at night to switch on the generator, we would lose lakhs of rupees in frozen foods. Till we could find someone else, we decided to retain him since the equipments had not yet arrived and we were at least a month away from our launch. The carpenter needed intermittent power for power drills or for sawing and the electricians for soldering. More often when one of them switched on his equipment, he realized there was no power.

Someone shouted Bahadur's name and slowly he trudged to change the switch. This happened quite a few times and each time Bahadur would leave cursing in chaste Hindi, creating a great deal of mirth.

In the afternoon, he left for his lunch. We knew that now we wouldn't be seeing him for the next two hours. So next time when the power went, one of the carpenters shouted his assistant to go and change the switch. This assistant was a young sixteen year old boy.

The generator was in the basement which was two levels below our store. There was a lift which couldn't be used now. It would take at least fifteen minutes for the boy to go down by steps and return. So the carpenters meanwhile took a break to smoke bidi and gossip.

After fifteen minutes, suddenly the young man appeared, his face white, like he had seen a ghost. He tried saying something, but the words just wouldn't come out. He mustered all the strength he could and pointed his hand in the direction of the generator and fainted.

We all rushed to him. One worker splashed water on his face. I ordered another one to go and get a bottle of lemonade and some sugar.

The boy came back to his senses but his teeth were chattering and he could barely talk. He kept looking in the direction of the generator. We decided to go and see for ourselves.

He pulled the sleeve of my shirt and pleaded with his eyes not to go. I patted him and smiled assuring him that I would be fine.

The black clouds which had threatened to rain, now decided that enough was enough.

The rains here had their own idiosyncrasies. They never drizzled, they almost always poured. Also, one could never predict the beginning or the end. Sometimes, it would continue raining for days. Other times it would barely last fifteen minutes.

We carefully sidestepped the puddles, which formed almost immediately and walked down the stairs. It was dark. Slowly we walked to the basement.

Ram Bharose, was leading us. I was behind him. Suddenly he stopped in his tracks and froze making me bump into him. I cursed. Ram Bharose squeezed my hand and hissed me to keep quiet. At first I didn't notice him because of his colour. But then suddenly I felt the hair in my nape bristle.

Camouflaged by the colour of the background, a ten feet python lay curled near the generator. My blood curdled when I imagined Bahadur nonchalantly changing switches without as much as looking at the monster.

Suddenly Amar, Ram Bharose's thirteen-year old nephew, spotted the python and he shrieked running back. We, who had stood immobilized, ran after him, scared of our lives, not waiting even once to catch our breath.

We were panting as we came to our store. But by then fear had taken over the whole team completely. They were scared that the python might attack them here as well. I tried to reason with them that a python was the laziest animal. Before it even moves a foot, we can catch it. But that did nothing to settle their frazzled nerves. They left the place without even looking back once. Ram Bharose was very protective about his tools. He would never allow any one to touch them. But now his planer, his hacksaw and other things lay there orphaned.

I immediately called Mr. Shenoy. I had read somewhere that pythons were non-poisonous and to swallow a human being they had to be at least twenty feet long. But still there was the scare. What after swallowing half of me, he suddenly realized that he can't have the whole of me?

Once he was over with his laughing bout, Nachiket advised me to contact the local fire station and the zoo. I gently reminded him that we were in India not USA. He simply hung up wishing me good luck. I was now on my own, deserted by my team. ('We are carpenters, not snake charmers', Ram Bharose had sheepishly commented later.)

The news spread like wild fire and in no time, there was a huge crowd outside the building. The rains which were wreaking havoc had now miraculously ceased. All the other shopkeepers had closed their shops. The employees were happy to have a day off without their salary being deducted.

Soon the owner of the building came. This was not something that was new to him. He had lived all his life in Manipal. 'You know how Tiger Circle got it's name?' he boasted. 'There were tigers in Manipal fifty years back.' I had to remind him gently about the problem we faced five minutes back and leave what happened fifty years back for some other time.

He picked up his fancy mobile and spoke to someone in rapid gunshot style. 'Tulu. It's the local dialect.' He whispered. It was difficult to keep Mr. Shenoy focused on one issue.

After jabbering for another ten minutes laced with his trademark staccato laughs, he hung up. The crowd had gone all silent. He waited for the effect and then declared that a snake charmer was on his way. The crowd broke into applause. Even I was impressed.

He whispered to me that the crowd has to be dispersed. 'So let's go and have coffee till the snake charmer arrives'. By now he had taken the full ownership of our problem. So I meekly followed him in his big Volvo.

He was right. Crowds have a very low attention span. So when we returned, there were just one or two guys standing there.

The snake charmer was already waiting in Shenoy's office. He had four more people with him standing outside. They all wore dhoti, shirt and large turban. Tulu language is a very aggressive language and coupled with high gesticulations, it makes for a very high energy conversation.

Shenoy smiled as they left, assuring me that these guys would be taking care of the python and everything would be normal. I asked him shouldn't we be informing the local forest range officer and the zoo. After all they would know what to do with it. He looked at me as if I was talking in Zulu. He brushed me aside saying that the snake charmer would take care. We need not worry.

He then excused himself leaving me with my demons. They gave me company for two hours – those demons. Just when I was about to give up and go home I heard something like a gunshot and then there was a huge commotion.

I looked out. The five men were dragging out that monster. I admired their courage. Imagine handling a live python. But then what will they do with him? There were no government officers? I smiled. Snakes were worshipped in India. I was sure they would leave him deep in the forest.

They were bringing him out tail first. It was an amazing experience watching the python. He must have been at least ten feet in length, twenty inches in thickness and must be weighing around forty-five kgs. I was bristling with fear but at the same time I watched fascinated. The python had the most amazing skin. It looked like a glossy mosaic.

Four people were struggling hard to pull him. It kept slithering out of their hand. Whenever it slipped, someone shrieked from the crowd. Finally the python was brought out and laid on the floor. Then I froze. The head of the creature was mangled. Someone was explaining that it had five noses. So it must be about five years old. But I wasn't listening. Furiously I demanded why was he killed. Everyone looked at me strangely. Why not?

This python would fetch the snake charmer at least twenty thousand rupees in the local market. Some smuggler would buy it. He could sell the gall bladder for forty thousand. The skin would easily sell for twenty five thousand. One old man in the crowd whispered that the snake charmer may pay Shenoy five thousand rupees for allowing him to take the animal. I was too shocked to react. Yet I preferred to keep quiet. I was any way never known for bravery. I can't recall having fought for a cause. A dead python was certainly not something to fight for. Besides, I was in a new place and in a minority. I had come here to do business and that's what I should be doing.

So I took a deep breath, gulped down my anger and frustration with some water from my bottle and went off to search the workers.

But the sight of the python had terribly shaken the boys. They didn't want to work here anymore and had apparently decided to quit.

Ram Bharose bribed them in the only way he knew. He took them for a movie. I was left with nothing much to do. The cold blooded killing of the python had shaken me. I went to the Blue Water and had a drink.

There was a cricket match going on. I hadn't watched a match for ages. Once upon a time I never used to miss a single match. The Australians were playing the South Africans. For an Indian fan, the Australian team was the most hated team after the Pakistani team. Hating the Pakistani had a reason. Politics and animosity off the field spilled onto the field. Before the partition they were a part of India. The bloody partition left a lot of bad blood between the two countries. But with Australia there was no reason. They were a far better team. But, every time an Australian misfielded or a South African batsman smacked the ball hard, a cheer erupted in the bar. The horror of the morning forgotten, I was enjoying the evening, soaking myself in the atmosphere.

When I returned to my apartment, suddenly the python came back again to haunt me, as if I was responsible for its death. The snake charmer, the real culprit, or Shenoy, the mini culprit, had no guilt. They must have had a hearty meal after getting totally sozzled whereas here I was getting pangs of unsolicited guilt. I tried to shake off the feeling and go back to sleep.

There is a myth that if you kill a snake, it's mate will follow you and take revenge. The python kept coming in my dreams in various forms and sizes. It was difficult to say if it was a male or a female.

The next day I went to the pizzeria with a lot of trepidation not sure of how many of my staff would be there. Luckily not much collateral damage had been done. Only Amar quit, which was not a very big loss. He was only a helper. We could arrange a helper locally.

I saw Bahadur and smiled. He did have his strong points. We couldn't fire him.

We had to finish the kitchen plumbing, air-conditioning, the interiors including the painting within fifteen days. The equipment would start coming any time after that. The plumbing was going on fine. The guy doing the interiors had a problem. His wife was pregnant and would deliver any moment. I was furious and wanted to tell him that even we were expecting him to deliver. The air-conditioning engineer had arrived and was busy taking measurements for the ducting. He promised me that he would finish the work within ten days. We couldn't start the painting till he had completed the ducting and the false roofing was closed.

Our Project Manager was expected any moment. He was a retired army officer. I was waiting anxiously for him because

I couldn't read drawings. So I was always filled with terror if either the carpenter or the plumber or the air-conditioning engineer had a doubt, there was no one to take it. I had already once made a fool of myself. The gas bank was in the basement and scaffolding had to be provided for the workers to erect the ducting. I had no idea what that meant.

Naturally when the scaffolding arrived, I expected the company to send one of their fitters to do the job. I was not aware that we had to specially request them for the same. So the scaffolding arrived minus the fitter.

I was curious to see what exactly was a scaffolding. What I saw instead was rows and rows of tubular pipes. There were some tools. I picked up one. 'Monkey wrench' our plumber added helpfully. He could as well have shown me a monkey's ass!

The workers were rolling on the floor laughing as I valiantly tried to fit the jigsaw. I should have been more discreet. Then they may have not realized how ignorant I was. But then I was anxious to get the work done as fast as possible. What they thought about me didn't matter. After all I was shelling my millions not they.

The Project Manager arrived shortly. I was delighted to see him. He brought the much needed army discipline and urgency in the workers.

'Your owner is shelling out his hard earned money, please don't waste it.' He used to use this line at least three to four times in a day. The workers respected him not only for his age, but because of his knowledge as well. Suddenly there were less biological breaks and the number of working hours also increased. I looked at him with the same affection that a rich lady looks at her poodle. Only in this case it was a ferocious bull dog.

His arrival now left me with a lot of free time. I once again started socializing with Avantika and her friends. One evening Avantika ordered me to come a bit early. I asked her if there was any occasion. 'I want to take you to our secret hideout,' she said happily.

This secret hideout was about four miles from the city. After crossing 'Blue Water', there was a temple road on the northeast about two miles away. We were on bikes since a car couldn't reach their hideout. After barely 300 metres, there was a narrow walkway. Some construction workers were busy constructing a house. We crossed the house and reached a dead end.

I gasped when I saw the view. It was simply breathtaking. There was a bridge over a flowing river. There were makeshift steps to reach the bridge. We all trooped up. It was actually a railway line. The view from up was panoramic. Tall and majestic coconut and banana trees lined the bank of the river. A couple of small fishing boats were returning with their catch. There were some bushes growing right inside the river.

We heard the whistle of an approaching train. All the guys shrieked in delight. I was pulled back by Avantika anxiously as the train speeded towards us. I was told to hang on to the side of the bridge. When I looked down, I almost felt giddy. A slip meant falling straight into the flowing river. Our hair flew wildly as the train sped by. It was so close that we could almost feel the train. It was foolish but very thrilling. The group was screaming with delight.

After the train left I walked on the track towards the makeshift steps. Avantika tapped me on my shoulder and pointed towards the center of the bridge.

We all were now walking towards the centre. When we reached there, one by one everyone started walking down the support carefully. These guys were real crazy, I laughed. There hidden from the outside was a small cave like hideout. There was some wild growth there. The ground was hard but not much dusty because of the wild grass.

Ameya lit a joint. The boys spread their jackets on the ground and we all settled on it. Avantika sat close to me. I smelt her freshly washed hair as I protectively circled my arms around her. We all sat there silently listening to the 'unchained melody', watching the crimson sun slowly set into the river. I didn't want the night to end. But it was risky sitting there for long.

When we returned I got the good news that the oven had arrived in Mumbai and would be transported to Manipal within a fortnight. This news really warmed my heart. The oven was the heart of the restaurant. Without it, there would be no pizza. We all galvanized into action. There was no room for any relaxation now. The kitchen had to be made ready.

Late in the night, I carried a few beer bottles and sneaked up onto the terrace. The night was young and attractive as if wearing a black gown embellished with twinkling stars. I was enjoying the bliss of solitude. I was feeling so happy. Things were moving fast. We should be able to complete the project as per our schedule. I was madly in love with Avantika and she too had come close to me. I could now meet her any time.

Suddenly I saw a falling star. I crossed my fingers and said to myself, 'Make a wish. Make a wish!' However, I couldn't think of anything I wanted. I had everything that would make one happy. I sighed. I will have to take a rain check, I thought happily.

I kept watching the stars till my eyelids started drooping. When I slept, there were still stars in my eyes.

✦

Time flew as if on wings. But our work also tried to keep pace. It was heartening to see everyone put in their best efforts. There was utter chaos everywhere. But there was some sense in the chaos. While the tiles were being fixed, the electrician finished the wiring; the painter gave the first coat of paint while the air-conditioning engineer laid the ducting. Every work had to be carefully monitored and synchronized in such a way that the other works didn't suffer.

The three thousand feet space was like an ogre. Each day there used to be truckloads of material coming and within a week it was gobbled up. The ducting, the chute, the wirings all went inside the walls or the ceiling and were not visible anymore.

Ignorance can sometimes be bliss. If we had even a tenth of the knowledge of the engineering involved, we would perhaps have backed out. One day we would proudly see this monument as a living testimony to our foolishness and ignorance.

One day a monster truck arrived. There was a huge commotion. Finally the ovens had arrived. There were two of them.

When we saw the size of the ovens, our hearts sank. The ovens had been packed in huge wooden crates making them very bulky. We immediately needed some labourers to unload them. When I called Nachiket, he suggested we use a crane. But the space was too narrow. So we urgently arranged some labourers. One look at them, I was sure that they had no experience. Ganesh was also a civil engineer. But his expertise was not heavy machines. They used their collective brains and after a long discussion tied the oven with intricate rope knots each carrying a bar or a rod.

Everything was going on fine when suddenly a worker lost his balance and fell. The oven slipped and was hanging on the railing like a cantilever. There was a collective gasp. Everyone was looking at each other for some idea. There was none.

In India it doesn't need anything big to attract a crowd. This was definitely out of the ordinary. A crowd was slowly forming outside. There were unsolicited advises but none even half intelligent. Ganesh was explaining that it was the delicate position of the oven which was worrisome. If it fell, there was little hope of its recovery. My heart sank. It was insured yet the insurance company would not pay the entire amount. Also we would lose valuable time.

Suddenly a group of eunuchs arrived, all garishly dressed and carrying drums. The eunuchs or *hijras* are an important part of the Indian milieu. They are the third sex whose signature loud clapping, exaggerated mannerisms and garish dresses attract a huge crowd wherever they go. They normally come during births or weddings. But these days they too had become commercial. They came here every month to collect some money from all commercial establishments. It was an extortion of sort. If not paid, they would hurl the choicest abuses and lift their saris and show their 'manhood', embarrassing the shopkeepers and repulsing their customers.

I had no such worries. My store was still under construction. They could show whatever they wanted. But still I paid them. Somewhere I felt sorry for them. They were not what they were because of their choice. So I paid them whenever they came.

But today I was in no mood. I was in a hole and needed whatever support I could.

Suddenly their senior-most member Shabnam Mausi came forward and asked me if I needed help. I was aghast. When such an experienced engineer like Ganesh was failing what could I expect from them? I was polite. I thanked them for their kindness and told them that we could manage.

But they didn't even bother to nod at me. They were looking at the oven closely. Suddenly one of them spoke something to his colleague and in minutes she was gone only to come back with a middle-aged Sikh. This man was a top erection and commissioning engineer and was working close by. The *hijras* had visited that site the other day and knew about him. We were formally introduced to Mr. Singh. He was a jolly man and laughed at the precarious angle on which the oven was perched. He had a very assuring way.

The first thing he did was retired our people and replaced them with his. Everything after that was a cake walk. I looked at the *hijras* with immense respect. They lived on the fringe of society. But today they had made themselves the most important person in our life. We invited Mr. Singh for dinner to which he readily agreed. After paying his labourers, I turned towards the *hijras.*

Shabnam Mausi in her trademark style clapped her hands and said, '*Chikne yeh tere par udhar raha.*' (You owe this to us). After that they took out their drums and we had a revelry for quite some time. We ordered snacks. Everyone including the *hijras* joined in.

I could now breathe easy.

✦

Singh regaled us with his humor throughout the evening. I was expecting a call so I wanted to excuse myself for a while. 'Singh Sahib, if you don't mind I shall take leave for a while.' Singh was in his element now, *'Don't worry ji, hum log mind karne ke liye kabhi mind istemaal nahi karte.'* (Don't bother, we never trouble our mind to mind ever).

When I returned he was recounting his journey from Delhi. Every one was laughing so much that they had tears in their eyes.

Sometimes even humor is contagious. The normally staid Ganesh also made us laugh a lot. Both the men were middle-aged but Ganesh had jet black hair. Singh suspected that he coloured his hair. In his highly Punjabi accent he asked Ganesh if he was dyeing? With a straight face Ganesh retorted that he was dying but he didn't dye his hair.

I looked at both the men with respect bordering on hero worship. These two were weatherbeaten men. Both great professionals. But I have never laughed so much even with guys my age.

When we were leaving I had one thought in my mind.

They don't make men like that any more.

✦

Man forms his opinion depending on the side of the prism through which he sees the event. Thus the same event can bear out two contradictory opinions. I had a very opposite take on the python and the oven incident. While many in our staff felt that these happened because we hadn't performed the rituals before beginning the project, I felt that these events had a positive effect and were meant to harden us for future.

The python incident made the staff much courageous. Now they were not afraid of anything. On the other hand, the oven incident made them confident about themselves. They had a feeling that they could manage any kind of problems now.

Suddenly I was made redundant. Each of my staff all of a sudden realized his responsibility. Now I had a lot of free time. Someone rightly said that an empty mind is a devil's workshop. This workshop landed me in jail. Avantika's poor friends too had to pay the price for being my friend.

Since there wasn't much work for me, my mind started philandering again. I reminded myself how much I had enjoyed that secret spot and requested Avantika and her friends to go there. This time they didn't sound enthusiastic. On deeper investigation I came to know that a few students had been mugged and one guy was badly hurt when someone hit him with an iron rod. He was in coma for some time and was recuperating. Because of this the police was conducting surprise raids.

I could be a ram when I decided something. Somehow I bulldozed all of them to go there. It was a beautiful evening. The clouds were dark and ominous. It could rain any time. It added to the adventure. Ameya made one last ditch attempt to discourage me but failed.

We went through that dusty and weatherbeaten road, two pillion riders on one motorcycle. The road was bumpy but because of the weight on the motorcycle did not jump much.

However, one motorcycle had a flat tyre. Avantika said it was not a good omen. We should cancel going. I again challenged them. Since when had they become such sissies, I chided them.

I told the three to wait for us. We would return to pick them up. When we came to pick them up, a slight drizzle had started. The earth was smelling wonderful. I took out my shirt and was singing loudly. But despite my attempts to inject some levity, I could feel that tension hanging solidly in the air. We could cut it with a knife.

I was the only one who ran up the steps and walked on the railway track. The height, the breeze and the slight drizzle gave me a high. When the train came, I was the only one hanging on the railing on the side. It wasn't that fun without company.

After the train left, I signaled the others to reach our secret hide out. Forget about smoking weed, this time there was not even a cigarette available. I was surprised. What had happened to them?

We sat there for some time, the most boring minutes of my life. I repented coming with them. There was no weed, no romance. All they wanted was to go back. I was furious. Suddenly I became petty. I wanted to enjoy their discomfort. So I decided to delay going back on one pretext or the other.

Suddenly there was a commotion. I joked that the cops had come to pick us up. The joke turned prophetic. The heavy police boot steps were coming nearer. Someone was rudely talking to the other guy with him. I was suddenly dumbstruck. Perhaps they were right.

There were two of them. One was tall and obviously the boss. He had very menacing moustaches. His deputy looked like a new recruit.

The man barked orders to his deputy in Tulu. It was obvious that he was asking him to arrest all of us. I decided to act.

I stood up all of my full five feet five inches height and with whatever dignity that tiny frame could muster, I went to the inspector and started talking to him authoritatively. I told him that we were free citizens and we could go wherever we liked. He had no business coming here and disturbing our peace as long as we were not doing anything illegal. We could sue him if he was not careful, I warned.

I was stunned by his reaction. The slap was resounding. We could hear its echo. My ear was singing as stars danced in front of my eyes.

*'M********. Saala, rules sikhata hai!'* (*$#%! teaching me rules). He spat.

I heard a muffled snigger. Someone from the group laughed. I was livid. This was my moment. Either I get back or my respect would be gone forever.

I warned the inspector again. But the unfazed inspector decided his lathi should do the talking. He turned me around and with one swift stroke smacked me on my butt. I screamed. The others were silent.

When the inspector noted satisfactorily that there was no more dissenting voice, he signaled to his deputy to haul us inside the vehicle as he took the wheels.

The police station was a nondescript small building. It wasn't surprising since the crime rate in Manipal was very low.

After the reception, there was a small room which I presumed must be the inspector's office. We were escorted to a room besides a large room which was secured by steel grills. It was supposed to be the lock up room. The inspector pushed us roughly inside but didn't lock the door.

It was pretty hot inside. We were sweating. One girl asked for some water. The assistant asked her to shut up. I had a brainwave. If it was time to make use of technology, it was now. I sent an SMS to Mr. Singh and Ganesh to come to our rescue.

Meanwhile the group had become restive. They all started shouting and screaming at the inspector. The inspector came and tried to shout them down. But he had underestimated the true Manipal spirit. The group out screamed him. Finally he was almost on his knees. This was Manipal and there was only that much limit that one could cross.

They shouted for water. He asked the sub-inspector to give them. They all shouted that they wanted mineral water. The inspector dug into his pockets and took out some money. Then they demanded coffee. The police station suddenly looked like a Sunday party. Furious at seeing his authority eroded and seething with impotent rage, the inspector directed all his ire at me.

Mr. Singh and Ganesh almost reached at the same time. Ganesh was happy to see Singh. He wasn't comfortable in dealing with such situations.

When I was summoned by the Inspector, I was expecting another round of violence. But he was now all syrupy. He chided me for not telling him that I was the owner of Pizza-Corner. Then he explained that why the cops were strict. There had been cases. Someone had mugged one guy. Another student was in the hospital suffering from multiple injuries.

I could imagine the reason for his sudden softened behaviour. Singh must have bribed him. I now wanted my dignity and respect back. I asked him what happened to my friends. He told me that the warden was on the way and they would be released soon once the warden took charge of his wards. I told him that I wanted them to be released right away. Mr. Singh gave me an imperceptible nod. The Inspector looked at Singh and then smiled at me. He rang the bell on the table. One sub-inspector came inside. He told him to release the gang.

'No, I will go personally with him.' I had to show the group my influence else I would be the laughing stock. Inspector Goody now had no problem.

Again rising to my full height, I went inside with the sub inspector. Their thirst subsided and their superiority restored, the gang was now silent.

With as much rudeness I could muster, I ordered the sub-inspector to release them. The sub-inspector glared at me, but obeyed. The Indian Police system is a strange system where the hierarchies were not dependent on your official designation but on the influence you carried.

Meanwhile, Avantika's friends yelled with delight and came out in a disorderly bunch. They all knew Mr. Singh and Ganesh and were pleased to see them. We all thanked the Inspector and the Inspector in turn apologized for the inconvenience. I could smother him for his hypocrisy. My face and my butt still stung with humiliation and pain. But still I was happy that I had the last laugh.

Outside, Ganesh still looked uncomfortable. But Singh was laughing uproariously. He had some work he said and excused himself. But we all would have none of it. We knew Mr. Singh loved fish as much as he loved his drink. So we went to Keydoor in Udupi.

The restaurant was full and we were a very large group. We told them not to worry. We were willing to wait. We reserved a table and moved to a nearby bar.

The evening went off pleasantly. When it was time to return, Mr. Singh winked at Avantika and me and said, 'If you feel like romancing, book a corner seat in a cinema hall. It is the safest place. This is what your Bhabhi and I did.' I couldn't help but like Mr. Singh. He was not just funny, he was a true friend.

The makeline, the slaptable and the cut table came and were delivered inside without any fuss. The accident with the oven had hardened the boys. They were now capable of handling any surprises. Luckily there weren't any.

The erection team got busy. But the light inside the kitchen wasn't enough. We had to stop the work at night. The electricians wanted to fix the bulbs after the mechanical guys had finished their work. They wanted to prevent any breakages. But now the time had come to fix everything. We had to take a chance. Too many people were working and the assembling work needed sufficient light.

Ganesh took me aside and advised me to call the interior decorators. The work was soon going to be completed. They could come and start polishing the chairs and the table legs and do the acrylic works and the usher stand in the parking lot. Shenoy had permitted us to use the parking lot.

Now but for any major disaster our pizzeria would start on time. At night suddenly we remembered 'O'. 'Nachu, all said and done we must give credit to O. Of course I am not forgetting your vision. By the way how the hell, you of all people, did the research about pizza? I am sorry that I underestimated you. You are a genius.'

Nachu looked sheepish. That was so unlike him. Normally he would swell with pride with any compliment. I asked him what was eating him.

'I have a confession to make Teju.' I thought he had screwed Shenoy's daughter.

But what he said made me almost faint. 'You know, I didn't do any research before suggesting a pizzeria. Remember the day you went with Tonsuk and I had stayed back, I went to a spa' I thought again he had screwed someone important. Nachiket and sex had a very close relation. But I allowed him to continue.

'There I heard an Italian businessman say that there are two businesses which can never fail. Porn and Pizzas. So if you want to get into business...' He trailed off sheepishly looking at me. I was dazed.

We had entered a business simply on the basis of a loony's comment!

✦

Mother couldn't move a step without consulting an astrologer. So before any important event Laxmi Narayan was consulted. Nachiket often joked that perhaps on the nuptial night, my mother would make me wait in mid-air for the auspicious time.

Any protestation did not dissuade her. Father would simply shrug his shoulders in helplessness.

Finally we gave up all pretense of resistance because apart from this quirk, mother had no other idiosyncrasy and we were allowed to lead our lives pretty independently.

We decided to consult Laxmi Narayan for an auspicious date for launching Pizza-Corner. Everything was almost ready now.

It took us almost an hour to reach his place. We had to walk almost three hundred meters since the car couldn't go inside. The whole place was much complicated than a honeycomb.

We went through a few narrow alleys turning the corner every fifteen steps, till we reached a temple with a large courtyard. The main temple was on the western side with another smaller temple on the opposite end. We had to remove our shoes before entering.

There was a huge fountain in the shape of a lotus in the center of the courtyard. I had never seen water coming out of this fountain. Though sun shone brightly we didn't feel our feet burning because the place was cool due to large trees around it.

We passed the temple and found ourselves into a small colony. This colony housed the priests and other officials of the community. We entered a large house on the right.

A child saw us and ran inside to inform about our arrival. This house too had the same curious construction. It consisted of a large living room. A big swing dominated the hall. The house was strangely silent. There was no one in the room except the child. She led us to a room through a side door. There was another room within the room. Though it had no windows it was very cool. It was very dark. Someone lit the bulb.

Soon, Laxmi Narayan entered. He was an old man and walked with a stoop. He was clad only in a dhoti covering his lower body. With slow measured steps he entered the room.

Mother immediately covered her head with her *pallu* (end of her sari) and bent down to touch his feet. He acknowledged with folded hands. I followed mother. He touched my head too and mumbled '*sukhi bhavo*' (Be happy).

Before sitting down we waited till he sat down. Mother explained the purpose of our visit.

He nodded and slowly opened a drawer and took out a blank sheet of paper. I winced. From previous experience I knew that he would smear both my hands with black ink with the help of a roller dipped in Indian ink. Then I would give the imprint of my hands on the paper.

That done, he again very slowly opened two very old books of charts. The pages had become yellow with age.

I did not have to tell him my date of birth or time and location since he already had it. I was coming here since I was a little boy.

Then he marked the imprint of the hands into different areas and calculated the distance between the phalanges, the width of the palm and the gaps between the fingers.

We sat with bated breath as he continued his calculations. He opened and closed the books several times.

A little girl brought us tea in chipped cups. Mother smiled at her and thanked her in a hushed tone.

Laxmi Narayan didn't look up even once.

Once finished, he slowly kept the pen on the table, cleared his throat and sat for a moment gathering his thoughts.

'His business will do well. You can start on any day except on *amavasya* (New moon day). It was considered inauspicious in Hindu religion to start anything on that day.'

He asked us to hang a lemon and a bunch of green chillies, a traditional way to ward off evil eye. Also, I was to break a pumpkin in front of the entrance before launching. It was a symbolic offering of a human head.

He paused for a while and then asked mother to leave the room. Then with a solemn look, he turned to me and asked if I was seeing someone. I was taken aback. No one yet knew about Avantika. I nodded.

'Do you love her?'

Once again I nodded.

He looked grim. I was scared.

He wrote something on a piece of paper and asked me to recite it 108 times daily after my bath.

I looked at the paper. He had scribbled a Sanskrit sloka.

I asked him anxiously if everything was all right.

He did not answer. After some time, he asked me to call my mother.

Mother was sitting on the swing and chatting with the ladies of the house who had miraculously appeared from nowhere.

We left soon after. Mother kept asking me what he had told me. How could I tell her that we go to an astrologer for solutions. But today we had returned with more doubts and no solutions.

✦

We had a long debate on who should be invited as the chief guest for the opening of the pizzeria. Some suggested inviting a politician. We wrinkled our nose. The TV was on. Rahul Gandhi had vanished from the TV. That meant elections were over. He was now replaced by bald and ageing politicians going blue in their face trying to defend him. 'It is not his failure. The secular votes have been divided.' No one now gave a damn. Annoying people!

Politicians were ruled out.

The nerd suggested inviting the dean of their college. Others just booed him. When Nachiket opened his mouth, I knew what was coming. He had a one track mind.

'How about inviting this year's fashion contest winner? Better still, invite all the three winners.' No one could refute his suggestion.

'Give them honey and the flies would swarm.'

But I had another concern. We didn't have much budget left for publicity. We had already bought a huge helium balloon that was visible from everywhere in Manipal. We had arranged the mobile banners in a large truck. Avantika's friend had cheerfully agreed to distribute the fliers from that truck wearing our T-shirts. The advertisement in the local paper was expensive. We had no money.

I had a brainwave. 'Why not invite the owner of the newspaper himself. That way we can find ourselves splashed across their front page.' All the girls and boys giggled. I took it as an approval.

It was final. The owner of the local newspaper and the fashion contest winner. He would bring in the publicity and she the business. But there was one problem; the owner wasn't exactly a small fry. Besides, we weren't that big for someone of his stature to get interested in. So we had to approach him through someone influential.

Our list of influential people wasn't very large. It began and ended with just one name; Mr. Shenoy, our shop owner.

Mr. Shenoy cheerfully agreed. His wife and the newspaper magnate's wife worked for the same charity. So he would use that channel to reach him and then we could go and formally invite him. We all agreed that Mr. Shenoy was a genius in manipulation. Unfortunately the 'magnate' was out of town for the whole week.

So we decided to postpone the formal launch till his arrival. In the meanwhile we could have trial runs and a soft launch.

The trial runs were successful. Everything went off smoothly. We were told that it takes some days for the oven to settle. But the oven settled on the first day itself. There was no reason to delay the soft launch, so we decided to have it the very next day.

We invited our main suppliers, Mr. Shenoy and family, a few residents of our building and a few close friends of Avantika. It was like a dress rehearsal before the actual show. The guests arrived like they would do in any restaurant. They were received by the usher in the same formal way. The guests could order anything from the menu. Later they were asked to give their comments in the guest book.

The staff turned up smartly dressed and the pizzeria was beautifully decorated.

Avantika's friends knew about it but the students living in the building couldn't believe that they could order whatever they wanted and not pay. They suspected that there must be a catch somewhere. Maybe we would later hand them a huge bill!

I had to assure them twice that everything today was free. They looked at me with unabashed reverence.

The soft launch went without any hiccups. The response of the guests was positive. There were a few suggestions but nothing serious. After the guests left we called the whole staff, and gave them the feedback. After that we sent them off for dinner to another restaurant. We ignored Shenoy's advise and this time allowed them drinks as well. They deserved a party.

I saw Avantika rubbing her eyes a couple of times. They seemed a bit reddish. She tilted her head strangely sometimes while talking as if to focus. At the time I didn't bother much. It could be due to several reasons right from lack of sleep to driving without a helmet.

It was time for celebration. Avantika's friends were arguing whether to go to DT or Skylounge. But Avantika said she had a headache and wanted to go back to her hostel. I asked her to wait for a while and promised to drop her once I was free. But she was a sport and went back by herself.

Correa became a mini celebrity. He was flooded with several offers. He couldn't have found a better marketing man than Ram Bharose, since it was he who always was at the site. Ram Bharose was illiterate but he was not stupid. He knew his limitations. He could make anything out of a piece of wood. But that is where his brilliance ended. Business was something more than that. He liked and trusted Correa. So he referred Correa's name to them. They both formed a company and now decided to take up turnkey projects. Correa invited Ganesh. But he refused. He wanted to go back to his village. We both felt happy for them. They were the two most genuine guys we had ever met.

✦ ✦ ✦

VII

Shabnam mausi cuts the ribbon

In the end, we didn't have a formal launch. The media baron was still elusive. But the students weren't. They forced us to open. Nachu and I watched helplessly as the student power took over. It all happened suddenly. The next day of the soft launch, suddenly ten auto rickshaws stopped and an army of students entered the pizzeria.

I apologized and told them that we hadn't opened yet. They let out a collective groan.

Mr. Shenoy, who was watching the whole thing, came hurriedly and asked me what the matter was. I explained to him. He looked amazed.

'Are you crazy? You can't send them back. Don't insult Goddess Lakshmi. If she leaves tonight, she will never come again.' I was too surprised to react. He simply took control.

He went inside and asked the manager if they could feed the guests. The manager had a quick consultation with the staff and nodded his assent. Satisfied, Shenoy asked them if they could punch orders and generate bills? Yes. Was the music system working? Yes. Shenoy relaxed. It was show time.

Outside, Nachu cursed the newspaper magnate and commented that we could have formally opened it with the *hijras* instead. Suddenly I remembered the *hijras* and their help. We wouldn't have seen this day if they hadn't helped us that day. The more I thought about it, the more it looked apt. Nachu burst out laughing when I said I liked his idea.

I had Shabnam's phone number. I immediately dialled her and asked if they could all reach within fifteen minutes. I told her take any mode of transport. I would pay. We requested the guests to give us ten minutes. They were more than happy.

Very soon the *hijras* trooped in noisily. I asked the students wouldn't it be apt that instead of calling some inane celebrity, let the store be opened by the people who really made it happen. There was a huge round of applause. Manipal disliked anything formal and appreciated the worth of everyone. We were seeing living proof of it. So to a round of applause, the *hijras* cut the ribbon and began beating their drums and clapping and dancing. A few students joined them. There was much merriment and laughter.

I requested the *hijras* to be our guests and eat before leaving. But they lewdly clapped and asked me for *bohni* (the first revenue of the day). I joked that they were the chief guests and guests don't accept money. Shabnam again clapped her hands and said, '*Arre chikney, hum to hijre hain, hijre!*' (My dear! We are eunuchs, eunuchs.) Again the crowd broke into a thunderous applause. We started bargaining just for fun. Finally, they settled for ten thousand and one rupees. Number one is always considered auspicious. Nachu paid without any fuss.

Suddenly one girl spread out her dupatta and shouted, 'People, shell out money.' There was again a round of applause. Students started throwing tens and twenties. I truly felt proud of Manipal. With huge fanfare, this collection was handed over to the *hijras*. They were pleased as punch and blessed everyone and left the way they had come, singing and dancing. But their eyes were moist. They had been respected and treated like humans.

Shenoy, who first looked outraged, was now smiling. While everyone was enjoying he was inside looking after the arrangement. The staff hurriedly put on their uniforms.

He came outside with a broad smile and told the hungry students that they could now come inside. There was a huge round of applause once again and the students trooped in. A young girl requested us to play Cold Play. As the music filled the room, the dining staff became busy seating the young customers and distributing the menus. There was not a single vacant chair. News had spread about this unusual opening and everyone wanted to be a part of it. The crowd just kept pouring in.

The manager ran inside to co-ordinate with the kitchen staff while Shenoy took charge of the dining area.

Nachiket and I decided to take charge of the waiting guests. We had a few chairs in our apartment. We sent for them. I took a register and started taking reservations. All the while we were involving the crowd in lighthearted banter. A guy came in with a bottle of beer. He enquired pointing at his beer, 'Hey Buddy, can this go inside?'

'I have a better idea. Let this go inside you first and then you both can go inside.' The crowd broke into a loud laughter.

One guy challenged the tippler to down the whole bottle in one go. He took up the challenge to the cheer of the crowd.

Another enquired if they could eat outside. I looked at Nachu. He nodded. A few more wanted to eat in the open. Nachu immediately summoned a waiter and took the order.

The time cantered as if a terrier was behind its butt. Finally it was closing time.

We simply sat down on the floor too tired to even walk up to the sofa.

Nachiket giggled. We had never done so much physical work in our entire life. This was just the beginning.

He called one of the waiters and asked if there was a massage parlour nearby. The waiter shook his head. It was too late in the night. The massage parlour closed at nine.

Shenoy's parting comment was, 'Boys I had undermined you both. You are marketing geniuses. The *hijras* were a brilliant marketing gimmick. I am sure the local papers will be full of that news tomorrow.' It was difficult for him to understand that we were two simple guys with no intellectual pretensions. All the thinking we did was from our heart!

Before going to sleep I called up Avantika. She said she was fine. But this was the second or third time that this had happened. I didn't want to take chances. Tomorrow I would drag her to the hospital. Manipal had one of the best hospitals in the country. Avantika laughed. She didn't need the best hospital; just some Aspirin. But I would have none of it.

✦

But that tomorrow didn't come for a long time. Even when it came, it was not me. It was her father who took her.

My concern for her health was sacrificed on the altar of avarice. The crowds just wouldn't stop coming. We had never worked so hard. We stumbled from one day to the next. Our mind had stopped working completely. I even saw customers in my sleep.

We were not controlling the business but the business controlled us now. I am not a very tall man. I measure just 960.127mm from the sole of my feet to my butt. I had checked the length accurately in the mechanics lab in the college once.

This length is very important. It is the metaphorical difference between my life in Miami and in India. On any given weekend in Miami, I would be resting either on my butt or my back depending on whether I was in the pub or the beach. After coming to India, if my butt and my back were on the desktop, they would have been archived by now, so seldom are they used. Most of the time I am on my two tired legs.

We now barely had any time to meet our friends. We had stocked a mini bar in our apartment and scampered towards it at most midnights after closing the pizzeria. Our Kannada cook Anna left our dinner on the table. We quickly gulped down our drink, food and crashed.

The only thing that woke us up was the incessant chatter of the parrots at the break of dawn. We had opted for an apartment which opened towards the lush green jungle but we had not anticipated this problem. But now there was nothing that we could do. They acted as our morning alarm. In any case we had to be at the restaurant at sharp 8.30 am. The house keeping staff would come to clean it. The prep cooks came after that, readying everything for the cooks.

I took up that responsibility. Nachu was a late sleeper and for him rising early was tough.

He replaced me in the afternoon. After lunch we both used to take a few hours off and go back again at seven in the evening. The good thing was that we would never sleep hungry. There was always some order messed up by one of our staff. Either you had to eat it or throw it away. We avoided distributing it to the staff since it would lead to a bad practice.

We were enjoying too. The job had its perks. For instance, Our chest swelled when we saw a happy customer gushing that the food was awesome or overheard a staffer telling his friends that he works for a great guy. Young Rehan once mentioned that whenever his father was out of town, he remembered us.

At such times I felt a lump in my throat. It was worth all the trouble.

I kept reminding myself that I had to take Avantika for a medical check-up.

Unfortunately Avantika was free only on weekends. But that was when we were the busiest. Many times she came to see us but when she saw how busy we were, she left. I could barely acknowledge her.

Time was moving fast. The days were changing to weeks and weeks to months. Suddenly one night there was a huge thunder and lightning and it started raining. It was the signal of the arrival of monsoon. The sky changed from azure to dark. The trees had a freshly washed look. The green leaves became a deeper green. The thick bushes, pregnant with flower, bent still further under their weight. Men too were imitating nature. They were bending while walking, trying to avoid the onslaught of the sleet.

Nachu often got bouts of prose. He always maintained a diary. On one particular night he wrote

The raindrops, the ushers in the nature's theatre, gently tapped on my window, 'Get up lazy, you are late. Nature has arranged an orchestra for you.' But the frogs were looking for performers not audience. They croaked their mating calls, not worried about creating a cacophony and destroying the perfect orchestra, announcing to the world their intentions ... and their lust!

The monsoons have truly arrived.

But not everything was romantic. Because of the rains, the customer count decreased. Our deliveries were poor. I can say it for sure that the hospital was delivering more babies than we were delivering pizzas. I thought that we needed some aggressive marketing. So I decided to do it myself.

We had to face a barrage of insects in the corridor. Though we had air curtains, still some pesky insects would find their way in. The exterminator pleaded helplessness in controlling the insects in the corridor, who came from the jungle behind. The customers coming in soaked, would leave the sofas and the floor wet. We had to mop them dry before seating new customers. This extra work made the dining staff a bit grumpy. It was rare to see the sun. Even if it did come out, the angry clouds would cover it in a fury, leaving the world grey once again.

There is a saying in Marathi that in the year of the drought, there are thirteen months. We thought our year had fourteen months in the rainy season.

We tried everything but somehow all our marketing gimmicks failed before the fury of the rain God. We had to find a way out.

That finally came in the way of a bandh. Bandh is a very unique Indian sub-continent phenomenon. All shops in the city for no reason are closed. The people who call for bandh do not realize the inconvenience it causes to the citizens or the loss to the government. Bandhs can be announced by anyone. It could be by the ruling party or the opposition. It could be for anything, from a very important issue of price rise to a frivolous local issue of arresting a local goon. It invariably ends with a lot of damage to public property. Buses are sometimes burnt, shops that try to defy the bandh are stoned and trains are stopped.

One day a sudden bandh was called by the opposition party in the center. They were protesting against the rise in petrol prices.

We silently cursed them. Whatever little business we were doing even that would be lost today. Our staff who came for the morning shift were awaiting instructions. Buses were not plying, so the cleaning women did not turn up. I was feeling thoroughly depressed and there was a feeling of impotent rage within me. I told them to go back. The staff looked pleased to have got a paid holiday. I was standing there morosely wringing my hands when Mr. Shenoy walked in. He was somewhat of a local leader.

He saw my face and immediately understood that I was pretty upset to lose a day's business in these particularly low times. Suddenly he hit upon an idea. He came close to me and whispered in my ears, 'Look. We are lucky. Our shop doesn't open on the main road. Today all the restaurants would be closed. But a man has to eat. So what I suggest is that you keep the main door closed and allow people from the back door.' I thought for a moment. The plan seemed good but was fraught with danger I asked him what about the party workers who had called the bandh. Again he whispered, 'Most of this crowd is not a spontaneous one. They are paid by the party. They would be here maximum till the afternoon. After that they will go and booze. In any case, your business doesn't start before twelve. Today start it at one.' I asked him what if any of the volunteers notice it and came to damage our property. He again repeated that the parties pay these volunteers and alcohol is the major attraction. No one involves in these bandhs because of any conviction or principle. He thought for a while and then said, 'You can stand at the entrance. If you see a mob coming towards your restaurant, give me a call. I shall take care.' I didn't need any more prodding. I was now virtually running out of the restaurant. Shenoy ran after me asking what happened. 'The staff. I have to call the staff back. I sent them off.'

'Call them on their mobiles'

'They don't have mobiles'

He was much taller than me. He reached the parking lot much faster than me and we both dived into his car. I had no idea where I would find the boys but Manipal isn't a very large town. We saw them sitting in Tiger Circle. I felt guilty to spoil their holiday mood. But this was emergency. We needed business.

Till twelve there was not a single soul. The staff was cursing me. Around half past twelve, a couple came in. They said that they were hungry but all the restaurants were closed. I escorted them through the back door and told them that we won't be able to serve them in the usual cutlery. They said they were willing to even sit on the floor in the kitchen and eat. We laughed and I told them that they could eat straight from the serving pan.

Slowly, a few more guests trickled in. But the bonhomie didn't last long. Suddenly there was a mob but not of the dreaded kind. These were a bunch of hungry people. We were having a torrid time keeping up with their orders. But no one was complaining. I had another important job in hand. I had to keep a watch for the mischief mongers. Nachiket had already come and taken position inside. He advised me to stay outside. With a grin he said, 'if the rampaging mob comes, all the money that we made today would go into damages'.

I smartly commented that it was covered by insurance. But Nachu was no more a rabbit. He quickly pointed out that we won't get even half of the investment after the depreciation. I looked at him with renewed respect.

Suddenly I saw a group of men carrying their party flag approaching. My blood ran cold. But when they came close, I relaxed. They were all drunk and couldn't care less.

Normally business is dull in the late afternoons. But there was no stopping that day. We couldn't even give the staff a break. Luckily the second shift staff came on their own bikes and so as soon as the first shift left, the staff was reinforced. The customers continued to arrive till midnight. We had to close the pizzeria at least an hour late. By the time it was closing time, we had done the whole week's business in one day! We declared that the staff would have a party. A lady cooked from her house and sold excellent fish. They all chorused that they wanted *anjal* fish. It was a local favourite. We checked out how many guys drank beer. We ate and drank till the wee hours of the morning. Nachiket was grinning wickedly and asking when was the next bandh. Everyone laughed uproariously. We were happy men once again.

We always prided ourselves for having a great staff. They were not only hardworking, but honest as well. So we scoffed when the neighboring store owner warned us to be careful with our money. 'These guys look very innocent and are always smiling. But behind the sweet smile they are devious. They have no scruples and will steal whenever they can irrespective of how much you have done for them.' He didn't have any local staff. All his staff came from the north-east or Nepal. We had no reason to disbelieve him but we didn't have any reason to believe him either.

We continued to maintain our trust in our boys. But one day we did get a shock. It came by way of an email. It not only punctured our trust in them but showed us how gullible we were and how much yet we had to learn.

✦

It all started innocuously. Some boys from the local school came to celebrate their last day in school. They were taking group pictures. I offered to click some pictures for them since one of them would always be left out in the photo. The guitars in our restaurant were a novelty and the kids simply loved taking pictures with them in the background. After clicking their pictures on my iPhone, I asked them to give me their email id so that I could send them the pictures. They all were very grateful and thanked me profusely.

We were having our lunch in a small restaurant nearby since most of the big ones closed at three. This one was away from the main road and didn't close in the afternoon. While the waiter was bringing our order, Nachu sent the pictures to the boys from my iPhone.

When we were tucking into our chicken fried rice, I received an email. I checked the name of the sender. It was one of the boys. I didn't think much of it as I expected it to be just a formal thank you for sending the pictures.

Later as we finished and were waiting for our cheque, I opened the mail. When I read the mail I was stunned and passed the phone to Nachu. He too looked shaken.

The boy had written a long mail. He wrote that since we had been very kind to him, he felt it was his duty to inform that we were being robbed of our money. I wanted to learn who had betrayed us. I recalled the whole morning shift. It could only be one person. He was the star in our team, Sridhar. My heart refused to accept it but there was no one else today.

While reading his email, we understood Sridhar's modus operandi. When the waiter took the order, he punched it in the system. A printout came on the printer on the counter and one in the kitchen. The kitchen staff prepared the order as per the order. Once the order was paid, the customer got one copy of his bill with a 'paid' seal on it. The other copy was destroyed.

Many times the same table ordered an extra Coke or dessert or a starter later. The customer would then receive two or three bills stapled together with the grand total on top.

The rule was that no order was to be prepared till the kitchen received a copy of the order. But during busy hours, it wasn't unusual for the dining staff to shout out the order and wait for his turn to get his order punched.

This is where Sridhar cheated us. What he did was that he never punched the order. He simply put the grand total with a pencil on the customer copy and destroyed the other printout. A customer normally doesn't bother because he receives the correct bill.

We did some simple calculations. Everyday if he cheated on just four or five bills it could amount to more than thirty thousand rupees a month. If we counted the two shifts and about fourteen staff, it could be mind boggling.

It wasn't the money part that hurt us. What hurt more was that we were being ripped right in front of us and we didn't even know. The million dollar question was what action to take. We had to think carefully. If there is just this man involved it was fine but if there were more and if we fired all then we would be facing a manpower crisis. On the other hand, if we ignored this we were encouraging corruption. It took us a while to come to a decision. But we both agreed. This man had to go. But first we needed proof. We were sure that the proof would have been destroyed by then. 'Let's check the trash bin,' I said. But Nachu had a point. 'A guy who is stealing right under our nose must be a pretty smart guy. I am not against checking the bin, but chances are that he would have put that bill in his pocket and destroyed it on his way home.' I had a plan. This guy may be smart. But he had cheated. Surely he must be having a guilty conscience. We would have to trap him psychologically.

He was working in a break shift. It meant that he would return at seven in the evening for the evening shift. We had to take him unawares. Both of us waited outside for him.

He was a very charming guy with a smiling face. No one could imagine that he was a cheat. We felt sad to fire him. But what had to be done had to be done.

He came in grinning widely and politely wishing us a very good evening. Good evening indeed! I asked Nachu if he wanted to handle this. He immediately backed out grinning, 'Be my guest.'

I began in a dour tone, 'Sridhar. We are not asking you but telling you. We have incriminating proof against you. Today we have received an email from one of the boys who came for the farewell lunch. A few days back two Malaysians and one medical student had also complained about you. We had decided to overlook it then. But now we have proof that you have made over thirty thousand rupees. Now you have only two options. Inspector Gaikwad is on his way. Either you own up and repay that money or we will allow the inspector to handle this.'

He once weakly tried to cover himself with the usual 'We had wrongly punched one extra bill so I was adjusting it' excuse. I asked him who gave him the authority to take that decision. Besides if there had been an extra punching how come we didn't find any discrepancy in the daily accounting. He gave up. It turned out to be much easier than I had expected. I asked him who all were involved. Luckily his was a solo act!

He said he had made twenty-five thousand rupees. I asked him what did he want to do now. He asked me would I forgive him. I shook my head. It was sad to let your best person go. But there was no other choice. He said he understood. I gave him a week to repay all the money. He said he would need more time. But I was livid. I told him in that case I would allow the Inspector to handle the case. He meekly said then he would have to take a loan. I was not moved. I testily told him he could steal from somewhere else for all I cared. He didn't reply. There was a moment's silence. I wanted to end this ordeal. So I ordered him to return his uniform, keys and other things.

After a moment's pause he requested if we could pretend that he had resigned and was leaving because he found a better opportunity. In a sudden moment of weakness I wanted to say 'yes'. Then I thought of the betrayal and humiliation we felt because of him. I wanted him to be a lesson for anyone else who tried that.

We went inside and gathered all the people. I gave a small speech informing others that he was being sacked and the reason for it. Also I warned everyone that today we had decided to let him go easily but in future if anything like this happened we would have no option but to go to the police.

The staff was silent. Everyone was too shocked to say anything. I then dismissed the meeting and asked Sridhar to leave and never come back again.

He was shamefaced. While leaving he came to me and said a very weak 'sorry'. But I was in no mood to accept it. He quietly left.

The next day he left Manipal. We never saw him again. Neither did we see our money back.

He did us incalculable damage. We couldn't trust anyone after that incident. Now either I or Nachu would sit on the counter as far as possible.

Nachiket always looked at the positive side of life. Even in this episode he found something bright. With a twinkle in his eyes he said that were it not for Sridhar, we still wouldn't know how to operate the machine and our control on the business would have been partial.

But I wasn't amused. I would rather have been ignorant than having to go through this ordeal!

✦

Festivals are like speed breakers. They put a check on the speed of our blind ambitions and bring back things in the right perspective. We had forgotten what a festival was like. But something close to that happened.

One fine morning, we got a pleasant surprise. A large Volvo stopped in front of our restaurant followed by a BMW. We braced ourselves for a group of hungry customers, but were pleasantly surprised to see our dads along with Mr. Gupta and Ramchandran coming out of the cars beaming. I grinned so widely that words wouldn't come out. Gangadhar, in his trademark lungi, and his wife were waving at us. Our mothers were behind them.

The moment Nachu saw Gupta, he impishly asked me what shall we do about the spittoon? I grinned at him reminding him that in the club he was using the toilet as one.

We were overjoyed to see all the people who had helped our dream take shape.

Success can gloss over a lot of personal biases.

Mr. Ramchandran, the villain in my book, now seemed like our greatest friend. But for him, our project wouldn't have been such a success. We suddenly began noticing all his positive qualities.

Nachiket and I quickly conferred and decided to book them at Valley Hill. The men offered to stay with us. We knew they were trying to save our money. But we told them we could afford it now.

Later we decided to take them to Udupi for dinner. The men wanted a drink. So we decided that Nachiket would escort the women to Woodlands and I would take the men to Guzzler's Inn. There were times when Nachiket could show his softer side.

It was only after we had ordered our drinks that Mr. Gupta started talking. He came straight to the point.

'What do you think of Avantika?' I was taken aback.

'She is a nice girl,' I mumbled.

'I know she is a nice girl. She is my daughter, young man.' I blushed. He laughed his trademark laugh. Then he paused for a moment and asked me gently, as if he knew what was the answer, yet was afraid to hear it.

'Do you love Avantika?'

I didn't know what to say. I braced myself.

'Yes, sir.'

I was expecting him to explode but nothing of that kind happened.

'You know she is my only daughter. We have pampered her a lot. Will you promise to take care of her.'

'Yes, sir.'

'Hmm.'

Suddenly he smiled. 'I will let you on to a secret, son. Your father and I had agreed on this wedding long back.' Dad simply winked at me.

The older generation was wicked.

He suddenly changed the topic. 'Since I am here maybe I will take Avantika for a check-up. She is complaining of headaches often. I guess she has to start wearing glasses from now on. We are a family of Chartered Accountants you know. Probably it is hereditary.'

I kicked myself for being so negligent. It had been more than three weeks since we had taken an appointment with the doctor. I had clean forgotten about it!

Three is considered an inauspicious number in Hindu religion. Our elders were wise people. There must be a reason for it. I do not know whether things would have been different if only two of us had gone. But still in retrospect I often feel sad. I should have taken Avantika to the doctor long back. If the ancient scriptures are to be believed, somewhere I was responsible for the tragedy waiting around the corner.

Avantika, Mr. Gupta and I went to the Ophthalmology department of the hospital. We waited in the lounge as Avantika went inside to get the tests done.

After sometime the doctor called us and informed us to come the next day. They had some more tests to perform. We thought nothing much of it that time. While returning I teased her about how funny she would look in glasses. She retorted saying she would go in for contact lenses. I was imitating her about how she would lose her contact lens in the wash basin and search for them. She was playfully slapping me. Mr. Gupta kept looking at us indulgently.

✦ ✦ ✦

VIII

Disaster strikes...

The bomb dropped on us on the third day. Nothing could have prepared us for this catastrophe.

We could not go to the hospital the next day as we decided to go to Malpe Beach. Goa was just four hours from here. But Malpe Beach did not have any trappings of glamour usually associated with beach towns. There were no fancy tourists, no posh restaurants, no line of cars. But it was my favourite place. The water was clean and the waves were gentle.

Those waves kept us engrossed and at least for the time being protected us from the waves of sorrow which would crash violently against our tender feelings. Our lives was soon going to turn into a nightmare.

I would soon remember old Laxminarayan and his grim expression.

The next day we were informed that Avantika may be suffering from a rare disorder known as Chronic Progressive External Opthalmoplegia which causes slow paralysis of the eyelids. That was the reason her eyelids tended to droop. It was curable but it would take a long time. But again they were not sure. Since it was a rare disease they suggested that we should see a specialist.

Mr. Gupta was devastated. Avantika's mother started crying. Father and mother were trying hard to console them. But it wasn't easy. Even mother's eyes were moist. Avantika was brave throughout. She took it in her usual casual way.

'Come on mom. Its not the end of the world. People suffer more serious diseases and still survive. At least I am still alive. You guys are behaving as if I will die tomorrow.' I felt proud of her.

Mr. Gupta was silent the next morning. His eyes were red. Looked like he had not slept the whole night. I decided to leave him alone. It must be tormenting for him to see his only daughter suffering.

After almost an hour I went back to see him again. He was still staring into nothingness and had not moved even an inch. I thought it was now time for me to intervene.

I brewed two cups of coffee and went to the balcony. 'Good morning, sir. Just woke up and was looking for someone to share my coffee with'.

He nodded thanks as he took his mug from me but said nothing.

'Enjoying the sunrise? I think, it is the best sunrise I have ever seen!' He was still silent.

Quietly I went inside and switched on the television. I switched on his favourite news channel and raised the volume. Normally he would be attracted by the news. It was impossible to keep him from commenting on politics. But today he sat outside unmoved. I went back again and sat next to him in silence.

After a while he asked me, 'Tejas, what wrong have I done in my life? Why is my daughter suffering?' I kept silent. I knew it was a rhetorical question. He wasn't expecting any answer from me.

'You know I am thinking of taking Avantika to Hyderabad for her treatment.' I was taken aback.

'Mr. Gupta, no offense meant, but this is one of the best hospitals in the country!'

'Its not about the hospital. You weren't there when we met the doctor. It is a rare disease. There is not much research done. I would like to take her to a specialty hospital. We may even have to take her abroad.' He again fell silent. Then in a very low voice, which betrayed all the anguish he felt, he said, 'Besides she would be getting the comforts of home.' I felt sorry for him. I could see his heart tearing apart. But I have never been good at these things. I feel tongue tied. Words just refuse to come out.

I wasn't sure how Avantika would take it. She had her submissions within a few days. But this was a family matter and I decided to keep my counsel to myself.

As I had expected, she deferred going to Hyderabad by a fortnight. Mr. Gupta did not seem very happy about it. But he knew when to keep quiet. Mrs. Gupta had wept the whole night and had to be given sedatives and was still asleep.

Soon my parents joined us. But I knew my parents. They would never dream of giving advise till asked for. Mr. Gupta seemed to have already made up his mind.

I looked at my watch. It was time to open the pizzeria. The staff would be waiting for me outside it. I excused myself and left.

I just sat there numbly not knowing what to do. My life had suddenly nosedived. I was feeling a vast emptiness inside me. After the staff settled to their morning chores, I went back to the apartment.

Everyone, including Nachiket had woken up. Normally that would have meant a lot of ribbing. But today things were different. I kept silent. Nachiket's parents were staying in a hotel. They too had arrived. Nachiket had ordered some hot breakfast from a nearby Udupi hotel. Dad had become addicted to the local bread. So Anna made some toast and boiled eggs for him.

Everyone tried to make some small talk but soon realized the futility of it. The pregnant silence was more evocative. Avantika had a morning class and was supposed to come in the noon. I offered them to come and sit in the restaurant.

Dad joked that we would fill up three tables. I assured him that there wasn't much business in the morning, just a few medical students came in the afternoon. But they declined.

Nachiket and I were only too happy to leave. The tension in the room could be sliced with a knife.

It was a relief to come to the pizzeria. I sat down before the computer and started checking the previous day's sales. Nachiket went inside the kitchen and asked the product staff to do a physical stock check. They were taken aback. We never did it in the first week of the stock arrival. Nachiket had never ever been a part of that drill.

But I understood him. He was trying to channelise all his tensions into physical work.

I couldn't take the tension any longer. I made some tea and invited Nachiket to join me. We never had tea that early. The staff knew my timings. At sharp eleven, someone would come with tea.

As we sat sipping our tea, Nachiket was humming tunelessly. He had opened a can of pineapple and was absent mindedly eating canned pineapple and sipping tea.

He formally asked me what had the doctors said. I was waiting for that cue. Slowly I poured out the whole story. I didn't stop there. I also mentioned my morning conversation with her dad.

I watched the steam coming from the glass of tea. My tension which hitherto had frozen suddenly seemed to now thaw in the presence of a sympathetic listener. Nachu didn't stop me even once. I expressed all my fears and worries. The words just simply flowed out. Finally when I thought that there was nothing left inside me, I became silent.

After a long time, Nachiket asked me what was my plan. I hadn't thought about it so far. I simply sat motionless.

Avantika came around lunch time. She looked quite fresh and more relaxed than any of us. It seemed that she was oblivious of the storm created by her in everyone's life. We had a quiet lunch after which every one excused themselves, leaving the family to decide what to do.

I was sitting in the restaurant when I got a call from her. She informed me that she would be going to Hyderabad after a fortnight after her submissions. Immediately I told her that I would go along with her. With mischief in her voice she asked me what would happen to the restaurant. I joked that it is in safe hands. She did not oppose. I asked her to confirm her departure date so that I could book the flight. She promised me that she would let me know within a day or two and hung up.

Nachiket was very quiet after our telephonic conversation. Normally I would have noticed it. But now I was too engrossed in the crisis that had suddenly come as a stranger and now just refused to go.

In the evening we informed Mr. Gupta about our decision. He gently chided me for ignoring our restaurant. But I could see, in his heart of hearts he was delighted. I assured him not to worry and that our restaurant would not suffer even if I were not there.

He kept silent.

When we were alone, Dad spoke to me very gently, 'Son. I am very proud of you today. Your decision may or may not be right. But also remember you have a partner in the business. I notice that you never tell him what decision you have made. Always involve him in any decision making and arrive at a mutual decision. Partnership is all about understanding and giving and receiving respect. You cannot build a business on unilateral decisions'.

I looked at him with a new respect. He had never imposed his thoughts on me. But when it was needed, he articulated his thoughts in a very convincing and non-offensive manner.

I did not know that Nachiket was so sensitive. Little did I know then that my father was right. Experience has its own value. Somewhere I had underestimated the dynamics of a partnership.

Our guest's left us the next day leaving us with a lot of emptiness. I admired them about the dignity with which they had handled the situation. I thought about their capacity to bear pain without expressing it in any way. Also I thought about their maturity in dealing with various situations. It is these situations that separate boys from men. Mrs. Gangadhar hugged her Nihar. I told her I was lucky now that I had two mothers. She told me that my room in their house was always waiting for me. Mom looked at me with pride.

Mr. Gupta called me up from Hyderabad and thanked me for the support. I assured him that I wasn't doing anyone a favour.

✦

I was able to see very little of Avantika. She was busy with her submissions. I tried to keep myself busy with my work. It is ironic that when one wants to submerge oneself in work, there isn't much work. The restaurant was going through one of the lean phases. Rains mean not much of outdoor eating and so no business for us. I had to dig deep to find some work. I prepared various kinds of reports. I prepared our consumption sheets, damages records, each vendors' separate monthly supplies. Finally I couldn't think of any more reports. Then I thought of some innovative marketing strategies. This was an educational town and as such there were not many recreational facilities. All students did was go to the various pubs and get drunk. I remembered my days in the UK. Introducing BINGO would be a good idea. We could slot them over weekends during the afternoons. I worked out the details and prepared four alternative plans. Nachiket liked the idea.

During the afternoons business was slack. We could introduce an afternoon of entertainment. The entrance fee would include a Coke and some starter. We both agreed that the prize money had to be lucrative. We decide to sponsor the first few ones and then later if it clicked offer ninety percent of the collection as prize money. After deduction, it could be a tidy sum and would definitely be attractive.

We worked hard on it. After that not knowing what to do I hit the gym and worked out ferociously. After an exhausting work out, I took a cold shower. But nothing was helping me in keeping my thoughts off Avantika.

I decided to walk back to my apartment. I wanted to be so tired that the moment I crashed on my bed, I would fall asleep.

As I came out on the main road, I saw a procession. I cursed silently.

Four men were leading a funeral procession followed by a small crowd chanting *'Ram naam satya hai'* (only lord's name is truth). The stars too had conspired against me. Seeing a dead body wasn't the best of omens!

I headed for the nearest pub. This was one place that never disappointed me. Lady Luck, which had always been by my side, seemed to have deserted me when I needed her the most!

✦

Next day when Avantika came there was hardly any trace of difference in her. Only her eyes looked a little droopy. I hugged her hard and kissed her with all my might.

'Whoa! Whoa! Whoa!. Don't slobber all over me.' I laughed. Avantika was a doughty girl. It would take more than a silly illness with a difficult name to put her spirits down. She was a fighter and she would take the fight all the way into the enemy's camp. I suddenly felt very positive. She had only been diagnosed, but no one had said that it was fatal. We would fight it together! I may have faith in our astrologer Laxminarayan, but I had more faith in my luck and in my mother's faith. Laxminarayan was after all just a human being who had skills to forecast the future. That didn't make him God! There was a greater force than him, that would see that his prediction would be nipped in the bud.

All of a sudden I felt very light. The tensions that I was experiencing for the past few days seemed to have dissipated. There is no greater force than fear to pull oneself down. But there is also no greater force than faith to pull oneself out of the hole.

I wanted this feathery feeling to go on for ever. But I knew myself too well. The moment Avantika left, I would start to worry again.

I held out my hand to her and offered to take her out for a walk. It had just rained. The streets were wet and muddy. There were small pools of muddy water everywhere. We carefully walked on it trying to protect ourselves from the muddy puddles yet not leaving our hands. We seemed inseparable. I promised her that no matter what, I wouldn't leave her hand.

Just then a bus drove past. The reckless driver drove his bus straight into a pothole splashing us with the brown muddy water. I immediately released Avantika's hand and covered my face. It was a reflex action. Avantika burst out laughing. First I didn't understand the reason for it. But then she mimicked me, her face in mock seriousness promising that I would never leave her hand. Now I too was chortling with laughter. The passengers in the passing buses and the pedestrians looked at us with surprise. It was indeed difficult to understand what was so funny about getting drenched by a speeding bus.

✦

This time when we left Manipal, the mood was somber. All her friends were there to see Avantika off, but there was no cheering. Avantika tried hard to make them laugh but gave up.

Nachiket came to the airport. He was silent all the way. Mr. Gupta came to pick us up. We drove straight to Avantika's house. I pined for tea. But nothing in the Gupta household was simple. It turned out to be elaborate as usual. By now they knew my habits. So there were some cucumber sandwiches and biscuits added to the spread. Their car then drove me to my home. We decided to meet at the hospital next morning. The eye institute was one of the premier eye hospitals in India.

Dad and mom were pleased to see me. Mom fussed over us at dinner as dad and I sat and talked about Avantika's health.

I was sleeping on my bed after a long time. The smell of fresh linen felt comforting and in no time I was fast asleep. I felt like I had not slept for years.

At the crack of the dawn, I was woken up by the chattering of birds. I tried to sleep again but couldn't. Ramu, our domestic help brought my morning tea. He had been with us since I was a child. I don't ever remember having to call him for my morning tea. My room was on the first floor. But he could see my room from his kitchen. He would see the light seeping out of my bedroom door and come with my tea. I often wondered if he ever slept. I was looking at the family album when he came up. Each picture had a story behind it. Ramu kaka as we called him smiled when he saw the album. He was there in many of them. He tousled my hair as we watched the album together and talked for a while.

I had forgotten the warmth of a home. But I knew this was not for long. Now there would be only occasional visits. I had to now build my own nest.

After breakfast, we went to the eye hospital. It was built on a sprawling area. The road was lined with tall trees. It was the month of May and the trees were in full bloom. There was a huge park with lush green grass and flowers of various kinds in front. However I felt depressed looking at the people there ranging from age seven to seventy wearing green patches or bandages on their eyes. We went to the reception and introduced ourselves. Within a few minutes a young nurse called Avantika inside. It took almost four hours to perform the various tests. At the end of the day, we met the specialist. Dr. Prasad was a highly respected doctor. He was tall and slim and had a very kindly expression. He was wearing a doctors apron. He explained that it was a very rare disease whose course was difficult to predict. Some people may have mild symptoms while others may develop more severe diseases involving other organs as well. Also, since it was a rare disease, it did not have a fixed laid out path of treatment. Mr. Gupta asked him if it would help to take her abroad. He shook his head. It was still early days. Let the treatment begin. Many people lead a normal life after it, he said. We had a thousand questions to ask but the doctor just refused to speculate. He gently kept repeating, 'Lets first begin the treatment and then see how she responds.' We felt utterly helpless. The wait was frustrating. We returned back none the wiser.

We decided to leave it to the doctors and God and lead a normal life. While returning Mr. Gupta asked me if we should be happy or sad. I told him lets be normal. I wouldn't mind having a girl friend who squinted. Avantika hit me with the pillow from the back. After a long time Mr. Gupta smiled. I asked him about politics. He grinned. 'The elections are coming. We will see more dimples.' We both chuckled. Avantika asked us what this was it all about. We told her it was men talk and she shouldn't poke her nose in it. That cheesed her off.

We reached home laughing and joking leaving our sorrows for another day. While returning we made a pact. We would not sit and wilt waiting for the unknown disease to manifest. We would live a normal life and take it head on if it struck. The first step towards that decision was socializing.

✦

Communal riots are the most rotten thing to happen. It is a poor reflection of the society we live in. But it was the riots which brought me closer to Avantika. People may look back in retrospect and curse the riots for bringing so much misery and shame. But that particular riot will always be etched in my mind. It was the day when we made love. It wasn't my first time. Perhaps it was not the first for Avantika as well, not that I cared. So, let us put it straight and blunt. We had sex for the first time thanks to the riots. It wouldn't be a politically correct thing to say. But then we were never political animals. We were simply two love birds. We were not looking for sex. It was unplanned; just like the riots.

The one thing that separates Hyderabad from other cities is its remarkable tolerance. It is a rainbow city with a multi-ethnic, multi-religious population who have been living in harmony for ages. The biggest manifestation of this phenomenon is a large north Indian population who have made Hyderabad their home. The Hindus and the Muslims have lived together for ages in perfect harmony. Both respect each other's sentiments and participate in each other's festivals with unabashed enthusiasm. It was not uncommon to see the Muslim brethrens celebrate Diwali with their Hindu counterparts and vice versa. But some people with vested interests were making a career out of creating disharmony.

Avantika had grown to love Aalankrita. It offered us the much needed privacy. We both loved nature and this place provided it in abundance. So, it was just another day that we found ourselves sitting in the bar in Aalankrita unaware of the drama that would be unfolding in the city.

When Avantika received a call from her father, we did not think it was unusual. But he sounded worried. When he knew that we were away from the city, he told us to remain where we were. Shortly dad called me with the same question. When I probed him, he told that there were some sporadic riots and the police had clamped Article 144 which meant that groups of more than four people were banned in public places.

We thought nothing of it and kept sipping our beer. The best thing about love is that all other things seem trivial. After about an hour, first Mr. Gupta and then dad called up to advise us to stay back there for a day. Avantika giggled. It was ironic that our parents were advising their unmarried children to stay in a hotel together.

We enquired if they were any cottages available. Almost all of them were vacant. The manager assured us that there was nothing to worry here as it was out of the city and we were safe. But we had no clothes or toiletry. The manager told us not to worry. He would send his staff to the village and get us some basic requirements. But clothes would be hard to find. Avantika giggled and told him that she lived in Manipal. The manager didn't understand the relation but smiled and left.

We thanked him and walked out of the bar to select our cottage.

It was not an easy choice. Each cottage was equally pretty and was built in such a way as to provide total privacy. We selected one in the midst of lush green foliage, closest to the pool.

Now that we did not have to go back, we returned to the bar. I did not have to drive.

Both our parents were calling at regular intervals and updating us.

Someone had thrown the carcass of a dead cow inside a temple. The cow is a holy animal for the Hindus. This was blasphemous. Expectedly it had triggered passions.

Far from the city our passions were triggered for just the opposite reason. Our passions were triggered due to love and not hatred. Beer too could take some credit for it.

Avantika came and sat on my lap. Hyderabad is no Manipal where this was a common sight. But the bartender was an old hand. His tips came in handy from providing the best service and that meant making himself scarce.

So whenever he saw our glasses were full, he would disappear for a decent period of time handing us the entire bar to ourselves. It was a working day and hence there was no crowd.

Dad announced that curfew had been clamped. But the Police Commissioner was his friend and he had assured him that we could return by tomorrow and not to worry. We both laughed. We could stay here forever.

After a leisurely lunch, we walked out hand in hand. The bartender was pleased with his tip and invited us to come back in the evening. He informed us that they had a swimming pool as well. We promised him that we would certainly peep into it. They had swimming trunks on rent he assured.

We couldn't walk much. The beer and the sun made us drowsy. We decided to go to our cottage and have a brief siesta. This was a perfect day. We were like tourists on a vacation.

The bed was soft and comfortable. The linen smelt fresh. We snuggled and went to sleep. I cannot remember when it happened. All I can remember was that I was nibbling her ear and she was purring contentedly. Slowly she turned and kissed me languorously. Her mouth felt soft and warm. I held her gently as I kissed her back, exploring her soft body gently. We kept kissing and exploring ourselves wanting this to never end. I kissed her everywhere.

I had never made love to a woman. It was always sex. But here was a woman whom I truly loved. I did not want anything from her. All I wanted was to give her the utmost happiness.

Our love making did not have aggression. There were no crashing waves. We both led each other gently waiting for the other to catch up. When we came, it did not have a mad shattering climax but a gentle satisfying end. We both lay contentedly in each other's arms.

Sex has a soporific effect and so has beer. We slept like dead logs even as our mobiles kept vibrating. Dad had called us to inform that tomorrow we shall be escorted by a police jeep and we need not worry. Avantika simply giggled. We and worried? This was perhaps the best time we were having.

When we woke up in the evening, we had coffee and then immediately went to the poolside. Avantika avoided swimming since she didn't have a swim suit. But I had no such problems. I was a brilliant swimmer. But it was a small pool and there wasn't much that I could show off. So I just cooled myself as Avantika sat in the shade by the pool sipping a spritzer, made up of white wine, lemonade and a slice of lemon with lots of ice and making appreciative noises.

Later we sat outside in the open bar sipping scotch and watching the sunset. It was too early to blush. But the sun perhaps had a premonition that the sex would be wilder tonight because we were no longer shy of our bodies. It went crimson just thinking about it.

In the morning a police jeep escorted us to our home. We were feeling foolish. But dad did not want to take any chances. Luckily there was no one we knew on the road to see our entourage. We would have died of embarrasment.

Fortunately the curfew lifted the next day and we were free to fly back to Manipal. Avantika had to return to Hyderabad the next month for another checkup.

✦

Everything was going well in our restaurant. It seemed as if no one had really missed me. The rains had gone on a furlough. They never left Manipal totally. But still it was a relief to the denizens of this tiny town and to us as well. Business had started picking up.

Nachiket was relieved to see me. This was the first time he was handling things all by himself and the tension was visible. He enquired about Avantika. I reported everything about her illness as well as our brief escapade. I was expecting him to whoop with joy. But his reaction was somewhat lukewarm. I let it pass, blaming it on the tension of running the place.

He enquired politely about the next step in her treatment. I told him that we would be going again next month. He seemed to stiffen. Again I did not take it too seriously.

In the evening he avoided me. But then, he was seeing a new girl these days.

Just as there could be a hundred reasons to doubt someone, there are similarly a hundred reasons to give someone the benefit of doubt.

I had never had a serious fight with Nachiket. So it never occurred to me that he would be upset with me for any reason. Little did it occur to me then that my affection for Avantika was driving a wedge between us. It wasn't a wedge of jealousy. It simply was that I wasn't concentrating much on business. Nachiket in his new found role of a serious entrepreneur found it unacceptable.

Only if I had paid more attention to my father's pearls of wisdom!

Nachiket was seeing a very pretty girl named Nausheen, proving the adage that opposite poles attract. There was nothing common between them. Nausheen was older than him by at least four years, was a divorcee and the mother of a young boy. When I asked her why her husband had divorced her, she said that she had caught him cheating. But Muslims are allowed more than one wife, I said. Then what was her problem. She replied that if he had married her and slept with her, it would have been fine. But she couldn't tolerate him sleeping with someone just for sex. I knew she was lying. Nausheen was a good girl. She couldn't even lie properly. When she lied, her already pink cheeks would become a deeper pink.

Nausheen worked in a four star hotel in the housekeeping department. She was shy and very reserved. I came to know her story slowly and in bits and pieces.

It had been almost a year and a half since she came to Manipal with her husband. They had been living in Bengaluru happily. Azhar was working for a two-wheeler company and was a fairly successful salesman. Tall, pleasant and hardworking he endeared himself to everyone right from the customers to the senior management. Everyone predicted that he would go till the very top in his department Azhar would just smile at the compliments. He was encouraged to complete his MBA by correspondence and was also sent for several trainings and workshops. Their conjugal bliss was the envy of all. Things were going well until one day the management, pleased with his performance, promoted him as Assistant Marketing Manager and sent him to Manipal where they had opened a new showroom.

Manipal was his undoing. His personal life took a downward spiral as his career zoomed. The air one breathed in Manipal was spiked with heady intoxicants. How could Azhar remain untouched? Alcohol entered his life slowly like an ugly tenant who soon threatened to become the owner. It had all began very innocuously. First time he had a glass of beer in a client's party. What started as one glass became a bottle. Then the frequency increased. From weekends, it graduated to the entire week. Then from evenings it became a lunch ritual as well.

Things didn't stop there. Alcohol brought out his violent streak. After drinking he became aggressive. First it was only verbal abuse which soon progressed to physical abuse. All the while, Nausheen remained a mute spectator. She belonged to a society where a wife hardly had any voice.

One day he came home drunk. When Nausheen gently chided him, Azhar lost his temper. He slapped her hard. Nausheen fell down with the impact, her face badly bruised. The mark faded in a day or two but the insult that she felt in her heart didn't go easily. She was deeply offended. This was the first time he had used physical violence. But she kept quiet hoping that it was a one off incident.

Sadly it wasn't to be. The slapping incident erased any respect or decency that the man carried. Once the restraint was gone, the violence escalated. Now the beatings became more regular and that too more and more violent, sometimes whipping with his belt or beating with a broom.

This was affecting young Junaid. The naked violence right in front of his eyes was leaving a deep scar. He was becoming more and more introverted.

Azhar's professional life couldn't have remained untouched. He was getting up late in the morning, reaching the office nursing a hangover and lagging in his targets. Gone was the neat and tidy Azhar. In its place was a shabby, unshaven skeleton. The management tolerated him for some time based on his past performance. But soon he was given two warnings. When the warnings went unheeded, he was suspended.

One day she went to the market for buying grocery. Azhar had by now stopped doing any household chores. When she returned, she saw him in bed with a woman. It took all her mental strength to keep her composure. Soon this became a regular occurrence. She was powerless in front of this brute!

Nausheen could see the writing on the wall. She knew that now she had to do something. But first she had to become financially independent. She was not educated and had no work experience. Luckily one of her neighbors was a kind hearted woman who sympathised with her. She helped her get her present job. This job didn't pay well but at least it gave her a breather. Besides it helped her to keep her mind off her philandering husband. But it infuriated Azhar even more. He had now started drinking even more in the afternoons. When things became very bad, Nausheen informed his parents who rushed from Kashmir. But the poor peasants couldn't do anything. They couldn't believe that this beast they were seeing was their once obedient son. They were old and not used to handling these kinds of situations. When things looked totally beyond their control, they decided that it was better to pack and leave rather than go through this torture every day. Nausheen was left to fight her battles alone.

One day when young Junaid came back from school, he saw his father staring glassily into space in a drunken stupor. The child was scared and tried to run out of the house. The angry father in a fit of rage pulled out his belt and started whipping the helpless boy mercilessly.

When Nausheen returned from her work, she was shocked and furious to see Junaid lying in a semi-shocked condition. His one eye was swollen and his back bore angry marks. She screamed at her husband and warned him that she would call the police. Azhar stood up shakily and picking up the belt from the floor began lashing her with it. But continuous drinking had taken a toll. He hardly had any strength left in his body.

Nausheen, suddenly caught the belt in one deft stroke and turned the belt on to him mercilessly. Azhar whimpered like an animal. But she was blind with rage. She beat him until she could beat him no more. Then exhausted, she threw the belt and went to tend poor Junaid. In a way she was fortunate that Junaid had fainted. He didn't see what had happened. She hailed an auto and took Junaid to a doctor.

The next day she informed her boss, an Anglo Indian lady, Angela, about her predicament and asked for hotel accommodation. Angela was a kind old lady who lived alone. She told her that since she had joined recently she was not eligible for company accommodation. But she could come and stay with her. A grateful Nausheen promised her that in return she would do all her household chores for free.

When she returned, she told her husband that she was leaving him. Azhar was shocked. He had never imagined that his docile wife was capable of leaving him. He implored her to stay, begged her for forgiveness and promised to change. But Nausheen was adamant. When all his cajoling failed, Azhar threatened her with dire consequences. When even that failed, he uttered the dreaded three words, 'Talaq, Talaq, Talaq.' He had divorced her! – In Islam it is that easy to divorce! No lengthy courtroom battles, no lawyer's fees. Just utter that word three times and you were a free bird. Every married Muslim woman probably lives in constant dread of these three words. But not

Nausheen. For her, the marriage was over long ago. There was nothing to be gained out of a dead relationship.

She began a new life. It took her a while to adjust but not Junaid. He had the optimism of youth on his side. His scars healed much faster than his mother's. He accepted his new life as easily as he left the old one. If he ever remembered the scars, he didn't show them. His grades, which were slipping in the school, started improving once again. He now got B grades as compared to the lowly D's and C's earlier. Angela, her superviser, assured Nausheen not to be too worried about Junaid. He was young. He would adapt sooner than an adult.

Angela lived in a three-bedroom apartment all by herself. She offered the hapless mother one bedroom. A grateful Nausheen did all the household chores for her. She cleaned the rooms, washed clothes and cooked food for all three. Angela, being an Anglo Indian, her eating habits were quite different. Nausheen learnt to cook her type of food, leaving no room for complaint.

Angela knew that the meager salary that was offered to Nausheen wouldn't suffice to support a growing child and her. So she helped her to get a part job in the evening. The money still wasn't enough. But it was better to live a peaceful life in poverty rather than in the physical and mental abuse of the past.

Nausheen worked hard. It was not just a necessity but also an anodyne to lessen the pains of the past. It was not that she did not miss Azhar. It was not easy to erase the happy memories. Many times she would visit her old neighborhood and enquire about her husband. But the information that she received only hardened her conviction that what she had done was right. Azhar was a hopeless case. His friends had forcibly admitted him to a rehab. But Azhar had run away from there. It seemed like he had no desire to live. Although now she was divorced from him, yet she worried about him. She dreaded for the day when she would hear the inevitable!

One night as she was returning home from her evening job, she saw a police jeep standing outside her house. A cold fear gripped her. Instinctively she knew that this visit had something to do with Azhar. As she went in, the inspector stood up. He bluntly told her that the police had found a body on the highway. A truck had run over a man who many claimed was Azhar as they had seen him walking towards the highway. They wanted her to identify the body.

Nausheen clutched at her scarf and prayed as she sat in the jeep. Just as the jeep slowly curved into the main street and the inspector pressed the accelerator, he had to abruptly apply brakes. The jeep swerved and came to a halt. The Inspector let out a volley of invectives as he stomped out of the jeep and slapped the man in front.

Nausheen giggled. It was a giggle of relief. The inspector looked into the jeep. Nausheen shyly told him that he was Azhar. Even the rude inspector couldn't hide his smile. He suddenly softened and asked him to be careful next time. Just as he was about to turn on the ignition, he had second thoughts. He shouted at Azhar and asked him to get inside the jeep. He said that he would drop him home.

After a long time Nausheen felt the closeness of her ex-husband. She felt her knees go weak. But Azhar looked at her glassily. He didn't even recognize her. With a tinge of sadness, Nausheen realized that the man who now sat next to her was nothing more than a stranger. They dropped him near his house. He didn't even acknowledge her as he wobbled his way into the darkness. Nausheen softly told the inspector that they should send him home. 'Where are you guys from?' he enquired. 'Kashmir.' The inspector smiled. He couldn't afford to send him even till Mangalore forget Kashmir. Their department was always cash strapped. But he promised to call his parents.

His parents came again. They visited Nausheen and were glad to see their grandson doing well. They offered to take them both back. But Nausheen shook her head. She knew that they were poor and couldn't afford to feed two more mouths. She went with them to the company where Azhar worked and collected Azhar's dues and handed it over to his parents. The parents wanted to leave that money for the grandson but Nausheen refused. They needed the money more than her.

Next day she tearfully sent them off. Nausheen felt very lonely. She met Azhar sometimes on the way to her office or while returning from work in the evening. Her parents had died long ago. Now she was all alone with just Junaid as the only person she could call her own.

✦ ✦ ✦

IX

Cupid strikes Nachiket

Nachu isn't exactly God's gift to the heart broken club. Here was a man who was proud of the fact that he didn't cry even when he was born. He claims that the nurse got tired of slapping his buttocks but all he did was continued smiling. I knew his one little secret which I had got from the stud's own little mouth. In one of those loose moments after a drink too many he had made a confession. The only time he cries is during an orgasm. This little nugget was precious information for me to blackmail him. It was to be used only once and in the extreme circumstance to coerce him into doing what I wanted him to do because there was nothing that Nachu feared more than being called a sissy. He protected that little information as aggressively as a starlet protecting information about her recent boob job or the latest botox shot she has taken.

But strange things do happen. One divorced woman and her innocent son did the impossible. They converted him into a human being possessing emotions like love.

Many eons back, a dacoit who went by the name Angulimaal because he wore a garland of little fingers of the people he had robbed, turned into a monk because of Lord Buddha. In another period and another place, there was a robber called Ratnakar who robbed people to feed his family. He was converted when lord Narada asked him that the very family for whom he was stealing, would they be willing to share his sin? When they refused, he fell on the feet of the lord and asked for penance. He later became the poet Valmiki of the Epic Ramayana revered by the Hindus.

These two have been considered the greatest transformations in mythology. I can safely say that Nachu's transformation could proudly stand up to those standards.

It's not like suddenly Nachiket became a monk. He still enjoys his drink. He occasionally goes for a romp. But there has been a marked change in him. He shows a lot more compassion, his face shows a lot more maturity and he comes back home every night.

I had never seen him going to a stationery shop and fuss over pencils and erasers earlier. Also, his Sundays were spent playing with young Junaid rather than in the company of his weed smoking friends.

I first met Angela when Nachu and I were invited to their house for dinner. Angela was fond of gin and lime cordial.

It was one of the most memorable nights of our life. Nausheen was a brilliant cook. She made delightful kebabs to go with the gin. Angela was tired of calling her to join us to eat but she excused herself to cook dinner.

Junaid was shy at first and hid behind the curtain and smiled at us shyly. But slowly as the evening wore, his shyness reduced until he came and sat on my lap and ate with us. It felt strange but not unpleasant. As I saw Nachu eating kebabs with mayonnaise, my mind refused to accept that this weirdo could ever change. It was just a passing fancy which would fade with the passing of time. The probability of their clicking as a team was remote. There was nothing common between them. It was like drinking beer with soda. But knowing Nachu, even that wasn't impossible!

One day I came out to the balcony to smoke. The balcony faced the inside of the apartment buildings. As I was stubbing my cigarette, it slipped out of my fingers. When I looked down suddenly I saw that a pigeon had made a nest in the ventilator in the apartment diagonally opposite ours and one floor below us. Sitting inside the nest was a small white egg. My first fear was that it wasn't safe from the cats. But pigeons were smart. They had kept the eggs at a virtually unreachable place for the cats.

Just then the mother pigeon flew in and went inside the ventilator, which was a very small hole. It then started pushing the egg with its beak. I first thought it was trying to break open its own egg. But it was only bringing it towards its own chest. Once the egg was in position, the pigeon settled down over it for a long, lonely vigil. This sacrifice was borne out of love!

I suddenly felt a deep connect with the pigeon. This was the power of love! I wonder if a few months back if I would have even noticed it!

I worried about how the mother would both eat and sit on the egg. So I went to the market and brought some millet and kept them in the balcony. I tried to attract the bird with whistles and other noises, but it seemed pigeons are stone deaf. The pigeon didn't move even an inch!

In the evening when my friends came, they all were very excited to see it. The pigeon was still sitting there. Manya suggested we sit and have our beer outside. I didn't like the idea. It would scare away the poor bird I thought.

Avantika looked as pretty as ever, except that she now more often slightly tilted her head to one side while looking at anyone. It was sometimes needed to focus, she said.

As we were drinking, the topic of her treatment again came up. She was standing near the window. She slowly came up to me and threw her hands around my neck and said that we both shall be leaving soon for another check up. Nachu, who was doing his evening shift had just entered and was standing right in front of us. I couldn't therefore miss the expression on his face. I noticed a perceptible change. When he had entered, he was pleased to see the gang and the beers or to correct, the beers and the gang. But suddenly when Avantika mentioned Hyderabad, I felt him stiffen. Again I wasn't sure if it was his concern for her or anything more serious.

But once again I chose to ignore it. The girls breathlessly mentioned about the pigeon and its egg to him. But Nachiket wasn't interested. Suddenly a wicked grin came on his face and he asked if anyone had a joint. Nachu was like a chameleon. He could flit from one emotion to another emotion in seconds.

Soon he got busy preparing the joint. Nachiket did it with the patience of a Zen devout. His joints were the best and he loved rolling them.

I blamed the change in his expressions to the light. It was dusk and maybe it was just my silly imagination.

The next day I woke up early to see the nest. As I was about to open the door, I noticed from the glass windows, two pigeons eating the millet which I had thrown in the balcony. I decided not to disturb them and went to the kitchen to prepare a cup of coffee for myself.

I had been neglecting the restaurant for quite some time now. It was not fair. I decided to spend all my living hours there till I left for Hyderabad.

As I was about to go to the toilet, my mobile rang. I was pleasantly surprised to see it was Jaden from USA. He was calling after a long time. We kept talking for a long time reliving our days in Miami. He filled me in what all the guys were doing. It was nice to know that they still remembered me. He asked me how Pizza-Corner was faring. I told him about Avantika. Suddenly he sobered.

Very gently Jaden said, 'Tej, don't fuck up your present with the fear of tomorrow. You are lucky you have found love. Give her as much happiness as you can. Leave the future to the man on the top floor.' I laughed. Jaden was an atheist. He never called God anything except the 'man on the top floor'.

He went on. 'Understand one thing well, Tejas. Never make the mistake of judging the quality of your relationship quantitatively. People spend their whole life without having a meaningful relationship. You are lucky. You have one. It doesn't matter if it remains for your whole life or just a few years. Be grateful that at least you had one.'

I thanked Jaden for his wisdom and remarked that he sounded better when he talked rubbish.

He laughed and said he was only reading from a book of quotations.

I knew that was not true. He was not as superficial as he pretended to be. Deep inside he was a very sensitive soul.

His words were ringing in my ears the whole day. He was right. Why was I upset. Why was I angry with God when in reality I should be grateful to Him for having given an opportunity to love and be loved.

I looked around the restaurant. It was a busy day. There were many of our regular customers. I brushed off all thoughts and concentrated on work. These folks were coming to our restaurant and splurging their hard earned money to have fun and eat well. We had to see that they went back contented. I decided that I would make up for all the time that I had missed. My demons buried, I was grinning from ear to ear as I waved cheerfully at one customer. Life wasn't as bad as I had thought.

A pleasant surprise awaited me as I looked into the nest. There were two eggs now. The pigeon had laid one more egg!

Time is like a balm applied on a wound. The pain eases with the passage of time. Now everyone around Avantika had got used to her illness. They had accepted that it was here to stay, which was not bad since now it allowed her also to lead a normal life. I dislike the custom of visiting a patient in the hospital. The patient is every time reminded that he is sick and hence people are coming to visit him.

So this time no one came to see us off. We were relieved that we were going alone. We did not have to discuss about the treatment or anything related to it any more. We were sitting alone. Without a preamble, Avantika said, 'I think Nachu doesn't like your coming to Hyderabad again and again.' I was stunned. Women have a very keen sense of observation. I asked her what made her think so. 'Instinct. A women's instincts are much better than men's.' She smiled naughtily.

'And what does your instinct say about what I am thinking now.'

'Cheapster.' There was a boarding announcement and I didn't get a chance to retort.

I had a lot of free time in Hyderabad. I remembered the pigeons. With nothing much to do I had researched about pigeons. I was surprised to discover some very interesting facts. The male and the female pigeons take turns to sit on the egg. I had always thought that it was the female's duty to hatch. I felt a new respect for the male pigeon. He shared the domestic responsibilities equally with his partner. The female sits from late afternoon through the night and until next morning when the male pigeon takes over again.

This time on we did not take long. Mr. Gupta was thinking of having her transferred to a college in Hyderabad. Avantika was not too keen on it but didn't protest either. He was even thinking of changing her stream from engineering to something less strenuous. I didn't think it was proper for me to interfere in it. Avantika was a grown up girl and could think for herself. I wanted to be there for her whatever she decided. It just crossed my mind that if she decided to permanently shift to Hyderabad what would be my plan. Should I continue in Manipal and take care of the business or should I move to Hyderabad with her. It wasn't an easy decision. But the truth was that I wanted to be with her as much as possible and help her get through this phase of life. Suddenly business and money seemed less important. My parents were quite supportive. Dad simply told me to do whatever I felt was right.

We were supposed to leave for Manipal the day after. Avantika went for shopping with her mother. Mr. Gupta invited me to the club. I thought about our first time there and smiled. It seemed like ages ago!

Mr. Gupta was very serious. His exuberance had simply vanished. I felt sorry for him. I tried to cheer him up by discussing about politics but he seemed distracted. After some inane discussion, he suddenly asked me if I was still in love with Avantika. I was taken aback. What did he mean 'still'? I asked. He said after what is happening to her may be I had a change of heart. I was very angry. What was happening to her? I chided him for being so childish. It was just an illness. How did it change anything? He was quiet for a while. Slowly he took my hand in his hand and said, 'Thank you.' I looked at him. In the semi darkness of the garden, I could see his eyes were moist. He made no attempt to hide it. 'She is all I have.' I grinned and said, 'Mr. Gupta. Can't you be original at least for once. You have stolen my dialogue.' In his relief, he suddenly guffawed so loudly that he startled a waiter walking with the next table's order, spilling the drink in his tray. Mr. Gupta called the waiter and asked him to bill that drink on his account. The guest sitting on the next table had witnessed what had happened. He told the waiter to leave whatever was left in the glasses and get a repeat of the order and that there was no need to bill it to Mr. Gupta.

'Don't worry. Some day we shall get even.' The man waved good naturedly.

The waiter went away with a look of, 'Weird people all of them!'

As soon as we returned to Manipal, I went and checked the nest. I was pleasantly surprised to see that the egg had hatched and a chick had been born. I had never seen such an ugly chick before. But that had not surprised me since I had read before that it takes almost fifteen days for the squab to look cute.

The stock of grains that I had kept for them was now almost gone. They had made the balcony very dirty with the grains scattered and droppings everywhere. Our servant had not been coming since a few days.

I quickly showered and offered to drop Avantika on the way. She was in the meanwhile gushing over the birds. I dropped her in KC and went to our restaurant. Avantika had met Nausheen a few times but didn't know her too well. Naturally there were a hundred questions about her. But I was in a hurry to go. My mind was still thinking about what Avantika had said about Nachiket. I promised her to tell her the whole story some day soon enough.

It was seven in the evening. The crowd was thin. It had just started trickling in. Nachiket was busy in the kitchen supervising the staff preparing for the evening. If he was unhappy, he did not show it. I headed straight to the counter and ordered two teas. The counter clerk grinned from ear to ear. He was a good natured boy and was studying engineering. We knew that one day he would leave. Yet we had hired him. In this business getting educated staff was not easy. He spoke fluent English and did his work quite meticulously. The attrition rate anyway is pretty high in this business. There can be no guarantee about anyone staying. At least we were confident that whenever he left, we wouldn't feel cheated. He came back with two glasses of hot tea and kept them on my favourite table no. 14. There was no table no. 13 in fact we had deliberately skipped it. Each table had a number. Thus the ones in the first row started with no. 1. So the first table while entering from the door would be 11, then 12, 14 and so on. The next row would have the tables starting with 20. We always mentioned each table with its number.

Nachiket joined me. He seemed to be in good mood. My favourite Cold Play song was playing. I felt totally relaxed and nostalgic. I remembered that feeling when I went to Hyderabad. But now I was certain. This was now my home. I loved Manipal more than any other place in the world.

Avantika was curious about Nausheen. So I arranged a dinner for all of us. Normally dinner meant after eleven. But for Juanid, we left early.

We all met in a small Indian restaurant, Angithi. It had newly opened and was already a big hit. Their fish was considered to be the best in town. The only downside was that it still did not have any bar license. We had a very enjoyable evening. Junaid had almost forgotten his past and was chirpy. He was enjoying his school and had a lot of tales to tell. Nausheen was busy with girlie talks with Avantika. She was enquiring about her health. I was left wondering how much Nausheen had changed. Financial independence had given her a new sense of confidence. Also meeting new people everyday had removed much of her shyness. She was glowing. I just stared at her. She was looking so beautiful.

We were having a wonderful evening. But Junaid was yawning. He had school the next day. We decided to skip dessert and leave.

Nachiket went to drop Nausheen and Junaid. Avantika had now moved in with her friends in an apartment. So she didn't have the monkey of 'perm time' on her shoulder. The Hostel was strict about it. But now there was no hurry. We both decided to go for a walk. It was late in the night. A cool breeze was blowing. There was not much vehicular traffic. The road was almost empty but for a few late night revelers.

We reached the kerb where we had kissed the first time. I didn't have to remind her. She was smiling. I took her in my arms and kissed her gently. Avantika giggled and said, 'Tejas. Can you believe us sitting here? We can't do it today. You should be really stoned to sit in this stupid place.'

'You know if I had money, I would have built a Taj Mahal for you here.'

She giggled once again, that giggle machine!

That night I had a strange dream. It was a wet night. A night with shining stars and a slight drizzle. I dreamt that I was carrying her heart in my hands and walking fast, afraid of it being stolen. As I heard footsteps close in, I broke into a run. Breathless and tired, I had no energy left. The robbers were closing in on me. I started weeping and running faster. Suddenly I stumbled and the heart slipped out of my hands. The heart turned into glass as it fell, breaking into hundreds of tiny pieces. Through teary eyes, I saw the reflection of the street lights in the tiny pieces and felt a million stars smiling at me. I woke up with a very warm feeling. No robber in the form of any illness could steal our happiness. We would still keep seeing a million stars and still keep smiling

✦

The squabs were now pretty pigeons. They woke me up every morning with their tiny cries of hunger. I felt a paternal feeling for them. Damn love, I was becoming soft.

Nachiket was sleeping peacefully. There was nothing in the world that could wake him up in the morning. But now he had a serene peaceful look.

Little did I know that a storm was brewing inside him.

We had finished our breakfast and were sitting in the balcony with our coffee. Nachiket as usual was smoking. The nest was empty, the pigeons had flown away. Was it some sort of an omen?

Nachiket looked very somber. His eyes had that far away look. He was taking deep drags and making rings of smoke. The rings were perfect. He was a master at it! The last time I had counted he had made 48 rings from one drag. I challenged him to beat that figure. But he wasn't listening.

Suddenly he said, 'Teju, I think we need to talk.' I had sensed it coming. The words simply came out like a flood. He had buried them inside him for too long. I just stared dumbly. When he finished there was just the sound of silence. Sometimes silence creates so much of noise that it drowns everything. I felt a turmoil but my mind was feeling vacant. I had tried meditation for a while. In meditation, they train you to feel a nothingness which I could never achieve. There was always some or the other thought that stole its way in. But today, when I was willing myself to say something, thoughts just refused to form.

Finally, I mustered enough strength to say that it was the restaurant opening time. I had to go and open it. Nachiket was now looking ashen. Probably he was repenting whatever he had said. I gently closed the door as I left the apartment, my gentleness in deep contrast to the turmoil inside me.

I was replaying the entire conversation while going tothe store. Nachiket reminded me of our resolve to make this store a success and how now only he was working. I had to bring my motivation back. I could not sacrifice everything that we had built for a girl. It was okay to go once or twice. But there was no need to accompany her every time. Besides, she was not even serious. What was the guarantee that she would marry him?

He was tired of handling the responsibilities alone and that I should now think over seriously before going to Hyderabad again. He reminded me of the various crises that he had to handle alone. The time when suddenly the walk-in stopped working and he had to scout for deep freezers else we would have lost almost two lakh rupees of frozen food that would have gone bad. How he managed to convince a competitor and keep our frozen food in their walk-in. He reminded of the time when the compressor of the makeline suddenly broke down. How one day suddenly there was a staff crisis.

No doubt about it. He had gone through a lot!

It took me over a week to come to a decision. It wasn't an easy one. I felt a cocktail of emotions. Sometimes I felt indescribable anger, sometimes pity, sometimes I found the whole thing funny. My mind was like a pendulum. It swung from one extreme to the other.

Finally I came to a conclusion. I completely agreed with Nachiket. I had over reacted. There was nothing I could do. Yes, I was just wasting my time going with her every time. I had forgotten our dream, our basic instincts and was wasting time on a silly emotional roller coaster. I thought about the many hours that we had spent on the project. All the sweat and blood that had gone into it. I thought about our parents and their association with it. It made me feel very guilty. How could I have been so selfish? How could I leave everything for a silly thing called love? I chided myself for being so foolish. Nachiket was right. I was putting the entire burden on him. I remembered one of my bosses who said always take time to arrive at a decision but once taken don't look back. I decided to bide my time.

I spoke to dad, mother, Mr. Gupta, his wife, Avantika, her friends.

I took long walks alone to mull over my decision. It wasn't easy and I didn't want to do anything in a hurry. One day I suddenly remembered the railway track and the police station fiasco. I smiled and decided to go there alone.

A train was coming from Goa. I remembered the thrill of standing close to the passing train as we clung dangerously to the railing by the side of the track. I remember that mad challenge on who could jump into the river and I had ended up with a sprained ankle. I was reminded of the smoking session inside the cave, the closeness and the warm smell of Avantika snuggled besides me.

I went to the DT from where it all started. I laughed aloud at the Heimlich maneuver. Manipal will always remain a place that breathed madness. We were already crazy. This place fuelled craziness. Many memories came flooding by. The python, the *hijras*, the crazy launch.

I walked alone in the rain. I smelled the fresh earth. I waved at several students as I walked by. We were now well known. It was a small place with not many pizza joints. I had made up my mind. Now I had to find the appropriate moment to announce it.

✦ ✦ ✦

X

Weird people, weird tales
certainly uncertain
it ended as it began!

I chose the anniversary of our one year completion. I didn't want it to be too dramatic. It was just that earlier we had to plan the anniversary celebrations. We had to decide on what offers to declare, what kind of banners and hoardings to put. That had kept us busy. Also Avantika had her exams till then.

We sat there, the three of us in the corner, having our Last Supper together. Nachiket ordered his favourite Carlsberg and mulligatawny soup. The waiter was flustered. He asked if he wanted the soup after the drink. Nachiket nonchalantly asked him to bring both together. The waiter called the manager. The manager said he just wanted to double check the order. Avantika and I laughed. His weirdness always brought out that 'I don't believe it' look.

We both preferred Budweiser. Avantika ordered momos. The Manager was relieved. He gave one strange look at Nachiket before he left.

We waited till our drinks were served and the waiters had left. Then I cleared my throat. I didn't know how to begin. It was a tough decision. But such an emotional decision had to be made unemotionally. I began with a long preamble remembering the good times. I looked longingly at Avantika. Then I said that two of my favourite people are sitting here right beside me and I wouldn't know what I would have done without both of them. I stared hard at Avantika and said that now I have to leave one.

Nachiket looked bored. Avantika had a bemused expression on her face. I had never talked like this. Anyone else in my position would have been discouraged but I valiantly went on. I wasn't sure if Nachiket even heard half of what I said because he was too busy taking a swig from the beer and one spoon of his soup. Avantika was wolfing *Tangdi kebabs* now, the momos consumed long ago. I felt like I was speaking to a wall and the echo was hitting back at me making the whole monologue incoherent. But I carried on. I told them about the turmoil and my sleepless night. The only respect they showed was that they did not yawn. Or maybe they were too busy for even that. I decided to shorten my speech. I had taken a long time in preparing it. But I was stupid. If I had really known them as I claimed I should have known. They were heartless pricks!

I mentally threw my well prepared speech in the dustbin and curtly informed them that after Nachiket's outburst that day I totally agree that if I am a partner in this venture, I must take equal responsibility, else I have no business being a partner. So keeping this in mind, I had taken a decision that I was quitting. Nachiket has to find a new partner. Mr. Gupta has arranged for a client of his to buy off my stake if Nachiket agreed. He would be a sleeping partner. So effectively it would be his show.

Nachiket horrified, jumped, spilling his soup on his pant and letting out an yelp.

I looked at Avantika, ignoring Nachiket who was now drenching his pant with ice cold water. He was lucky. The scalding liquid had spilled only on his thigh! It would be too much to drag his attention from the more urgent happening in his groin than his life. I told her I was close to calling it quits with her. I thought of the project and all the pains we had gone together. I thought of our bohemian lives together and how finally we had found a settled life. I knew I was pushing myself once again to a life of uncertainties. I wouldn't know what the future held for me. Will I do business or a job? I didn't know. But I was sure that I wouldn't find a partner like Nachiket, who thought we were brothers because we both loved porn! But that day when I went to the railway track and sat there all alone, I realized that even if I stayed back, I would never be happy!

Nachu finally looked up. I detected a tiny drop of tear in his eyes. Or maybe as usual the lights were playing a trick. Or was the soup very hot? He simply asked me one question. Why was I selecting one over the other. Why not both? I could live in Manipal and still look after Avantika. I told him that I had thought about it. But the same questions will again arise. I couldn't live without Avantika. She hasn't even been diagnosed properly yet. It may take a year, two years or never. She may have to go abroad. I wouldn't be able to stop myself from going with her. So the same topic would pop up again and again.

Suddenly Avantika banged her beer so hard on the table that there was a silence in the room. The room so far was so noisy that one had to shout at the waiter to be heard. Now they were looking at us. But she didn't care. Her nostrils flared up and her eyes flashing she said. 'Excuse me guys. I am not invisible. I have ears. I can hear you talking! How can you be taking a decision involving me without even bothering to ask me?'

Then she turned to me. 'And why do you pity me? I am not dying. It is just an eye disease. Why are you making such a fuss over it?'

Nachu was silent so far. Then he cleared his throat and said, 'Tej, you know it wasn't that I was insensitive or that I didn't care. I was plain jealous.'

I felt a cold fear run through me. Jealous! Did it mean that even he was in love with Avantika. Why didn't he ever mention it to me.

Avantika, her anger forgotten, was now staring at him. He shrugged. 'You are an idiot. It's not that kind of jealousy stupid. I am fine with Nausheen.'

He slowly continued. 'Look, even I am Avantika's friend. I am close to her too. I love and care for her. But you guys behaved like I didn't exist. I was never involved. Never even asked to visit her in the hospital.'

'But...' I blurted. 'I didn't think. ...umm, you would...'

'What I wouldn't Tej? That I wouldn't care? Is that all you know about me? I was so upset. I was never a part of the discussions. All that happened was that I was informed. I was never asked. I was told. I used to feel so hurt when you both went and I was left behind?'

'But I thought you wanted to look after the business?'

'Business! Tej, since when did we become so serious about the business. Were we born with it? Remember Miami when you were down with flu? I had taken leave. You scolded me for being absent? Do you remember what I had told you. That for me money is only a means to an end. Beyond that it doesn't mean much. It was you who increased my needs. It was you who wanted to make money.'

I didn't know what to say. This wasn't the way I had planned. Both of them were looking at me as if I was the worst scum on earth. Here I was thinking that I was making a supreme sacrifice!

When things can go wrong, they go horribly wrong.

We have a long history of embarrassing moments. Me and Nachu. But I think this simply beat it all. If I could, I would have liked to gloss the whole episode.

Nachiket was sitting there all spent out. I didn't know what to say. Finally I mustered a sheepish sorry. He was a big Hindi movie buff. Our movie was almost nearing THE END. There had to be a lachrymose moment. He tried to laugh but tears came out instead. It triggered the same reaction from both of us. Blame it on beer or blame it on sentimental bullshit.

We three sat there holding each other and bawling like three hungry puppies. The crowd which had just stared at our table when Avantika had banged the table, were now openly disdainful.

Even in that high pitched howling I could hear snatches of comments like 'Jerks', 'People who can't handle drinks shouldn't be coming to bars, such idiots bring a bad name to drinks.'

✦

The issue was never resolved. Finally Mr. Gupta settled it. He told me that we should hold any decision for the next six months. If I still felt the same way, then we shall see. But what about the NRI investor? Would he wait? I asked. Frankly, after Nachu's confession there was nothing much to discuss. But I had my ego too.

Mr. Gupta gave his full throated signature guffaw. 'There was no NRI. I was going to buy the equity from you.' I was very moved. I told him that he didn't have to do it for me. He said, 'Look son, I am a Chartered Accountant. I am a businessman. I don't let any good investment opportunity go by. Besides, in this particular case I had a personal interest. This is a good project. You guys are working hard. I do not want it to go into a stranger's hands. Probably after a few months, things may settle. We shall know how Avantika responds to her treatment. It may after all not be that serious. Then you may want to go back again. I am not going to tell you what to do. But I want to keep it as an option for you.'

My respect for him grew. We always saw him as an oily businessman. But he had his principles too! He may have a selfish motive in protecting his daughter's interest in the long run, but he was not thrusting himself upon us. Also he too knew that marriage was still very far away. Even he didn't seem to be in a hurry. We had still not reached that stage in our relationship where we could talk about marriage.

I thought about Pizza-Corner. We had built it with blood, sweat and tears. I had got used to this way of life. It was scary to think of going through the same insecurities once again. The more I thought about it, the more I was confused. Mr. Gupta advised me not to tell anyone about who owned my share.

Also not to give Nachiket any false hopes. Just put any decision on hold. Chances were that I would be back in Manipal soon.

Having taken a decision, I went to meet Nachiket with a new confidence and a new confident swagger.

As I walked out, the power went off. But in my newfound avatar, I wasn't going to go back no matter what. As I walked down the stairs, I felt something soft. It was a dog. It jumped up suddenly yelping with pain, scaring me in the process. I slipped from the stairs and tumbled down. A guest had arrived in a cab and seeing the lift not working, had kept his luggage near the stairs taking one suitcase at a time. I banged into one. As I gingerly stood up, one heavy piece of luggage fell on my leg. I winced with pain and collapsed on the floor, my confidence and my gait had both fizzled into thin air!

The next thing I remember was waking up in the hospital with a plastered leg, bruises on my body and bandage on my face. Nachiket and Avantika were having a hard time keeping a straight face. I once again thought I had seen tears in Nachiket's eyes. This time I was sure they had nothing to do with sorrow.

It took me a week to get discharged from the hospital. My leg was covered with doodles and autographs of half of Manipal!

Correa came for a week. He and Rambharose had clinched a restaurant on a turnkey basis. He brought Sapna with him. We offered them to stay with us. But they preferred to stay in a hotel.

Correa was unhappy at the turn of events. But he was a mature man and kept his views to himself. When I broached the topic of his relation with Sapna, he was frank. 'Marriage, no way. Not because she was a prostitute but because I value my freedom. I am not husband material. Sapna knows my views and she is ok with it.'

Slowly then he turned towards our relationship. 'Teju, I know it is none of my business but what is happening between you and Nachiket? Remember it is not easy to get a good business partner who happens to be your best friend too.'

I could trust Correa with giving me the best advice. I opened up leaving nothing. I told him about my fears, my insecurities, about Nachiket's insistence on contributing in the operations and my reluctance to leave Avantika in her hour of distress. She may have to go to the USA if necessary and I wanted to accompany her. Correa thought for some time. Then he advised us not to take any extreme step and be patient till the doctors were sure about Avantika.

Suddenly he grinned, 'And I thought only I had the most fucked up life!'

✦

We were at the airport. Nachiket had come to see us off with Nausheen and young Junaid.

Avantika helped me out as my leg was still in plaster. Nachiket was pushing our luggage trolley.

I felt a lump in my throat. I couldn't imagine life without him. Good or bad, he always had been there for me.

We were waiting for Avantika to collect our boarding passes. Junaid was thirsty, so his mother escorted him to the cooler. We were now alone. We both felt awkward as we were not good at dealing with such situations. We both started talking inane things. First the anniversary celebrations, then some new appointments, then replacing some old chairs.

'Teju, I am marrying Nausheen.' I was startled. This was totally unexpected. She was not just a Muslim but a divorcee. An inter-caste marriage would still be allowed but inter-religion? Tough. Worst still she had a child.

'Have you spoken to aunty?'

'No. I don't expect them to support me. But I have made up my mind. I shall marry her. With or without their permission.'

I didn't think it was a very good idea. Marriage is a solemn act. It is not just a union of two people, it was a union of two families. He was the only son of his parents. He owed them too. But I kept quiet. My own life was far too messed up to interfere in anyone else's.

We were silent for a while. None had yet talked about us.

Then I began.

'Nachu. I am feeling very scared and lonely. For the first time you won't be there with me. I don't know what I will do and how I will manage. The future looks so dark.'

He was silent for a while.

'There was no need for you to sell your share.' He still didn't know that it was still with me. But telling him would mean he wouldn't prepare for the final separation if necessary. I didn't want that. Avantika's recovery would take a long time. We were not sure if she would even recover. I didn't want to be in a dilemma. Nachu was right. If I wasn't concentrating on the business I had no right to own it. But Mr. Gupta was right too. We had invested a lot in this project. This project had helped us mature into men. Tomorrow maybe I would want to go back. Hopefully, Avantika wouldn't be suffering from anything serious and she would lead a normal life again. Then she wouldn't have to take a transfer to Hyderabad. We still hadn't told our staff of my decision. It was between me and Nachu. Our parents had been very mature about it. Nachu's father was very clear. He said he would love me to be with his son forever but would respect whatever decision I took. I was indeed lucky to have such people around me. I suddenly thought of Mrs. Sehgal. I was again going to make her busy. Serves me right for not listening to her and her swami. She didn't know about the swami and me and I wasn't going to break her faith. Nachu and I smiled thinking about her.

'I am going to miss you.' suddenly he took my hand and softly squeezed it. I would miss him too.

'Talk about being scared. How will I manage? You were taking up all the responsibilities. Now who will open the restaurant in the morning?' Nachu could laugh even when he was stressed. 'Come back Teju. I didn't mean what I said then. Please don't leave.' He was pleading now. I wasn't leaving him because I was offended I was leaving because I knew he was right.

I saw Avantika. She pretended to be strong but I knew she needed someone who could understand her and give her strength. Somewhere we three were very strong in our own way but still helpless and dependent on each other.

Then he said in a whisper

'Teju, you know I too love Avantika, but please come back.' I was leaving my best friend for the person I loved the most in the world.

I felt Avantika's soft hand on my shoulder. It was time to leave.

Slowly I turned to Junaid and hugged him and brought out a packet of Cadburys. He smiled shyly and took it from my hand.

Then I turned to Nausheen and hugged her.

'*Bhaijaan* (dear brother), we will miss you.'

'Don't worry, everything will be alright.'

'I don't understand *Bhaijaan,* things were going so well. Why did this have to happen?'

My mind raced back to that moment in the Buddhist monastery. I remembered what the monk had said that day.

'We are born as human beings. That is the biggest punishment of all. Don't compound it by being sad. Accept what comes your way with a smile.' I suddenly flashed my biggest smile at Nachu. 'It happened because this man is a sinner. Sit down with him sometime and ask him about all the sins that he has committed. It is karma.' Nachu smiled back. 'Whatever sins I have committed were not done by me alone, You were a party to it.'

We heard the last security announcement. We couldn't wait any longer.

Slowly we picked our cabin baggage and walked towards the security check.

Nachiket and Nausheen couldn't go any further. We had to say our good byes here.

'Avantika get well soon. *Bhaijaan* take care of your leg.' She said pointing at my plastered leg.

Nachiket suddenly laughed. 'Teju. Remember when I was leaving USA what Duncan said "Dude, go break a leg." You had then told me it was their way of saying Good luck. You seem to have taken it literally.'

I laughed aloud. Stupid Americans. Avantika was now dragging me. I looked back.

I saw them leaving and kept looking till I could see them no more. Slowly I turned around and headed towards Security.

✦ ✦ ✦

Memories – SWEET and SOUR

1. PHONE CALL FROM A STUDENT

'Hi I am *** from block no. ***.'

'Yes sir, how can we help?'

'Do you have the phone no. of Ashirwad Theatre? I wanted to watch Agneepath.'

'No!'

'You suck.'

'Well we only sell pizzas.'

'Do you have Domino's number?'

'No.'

'You suck.'

'Well, we have the nos. of Dean and Chief Warden if it helps.'

'You know them personally?'

'Yes. The Dean is a regular and the Warden orders from time to time.'

'Bye.'

'You forgot to say something.'

'What?'

'We suck'.

2. ANOTHER CRANKY CALL

A lady phoned. 'I received this flier in the newspaper. What is a pizza.' I was nonplussed. I tried to explain as simply as I could. 'Madam. It is like a roti and served with toppings.' She was furious. 'You sell one roti for Rs.300!!! Cheats!!! Come to my house and eat as many as you want for free.' With respect, I have to decline your invitation Lady. I eat bland food. If you cook the way you speak, I am sure my mouth would be scalded!

3. FOND MEMORIES

They were fourteen of them on the table. They had not grown old, but had aged gracefully. My staff was virtually eating out of their hands, so delightful were they. As I ushered them out, one old lady thanked us profusely and asked if I would make a reservation for a future date. Ever chivalrous, I said what is a table Ma'am, I can reserve the whole shop for you. Her husband chuckled, 'You are a charmer. Thank God you are much younger. Else you would have stolen my wife.' I looked at him. He was much more handsome than me even today. God, why did you stop making people like him?

4. KIDS SHOW THEY ARE MORE MATURE

The woman complained, 'This doesn't taste like cheese burst' To which I cheekily replied,' because this is Pizza-Corner and not Domino's'.

Her daughter giggled and said, 'That's my mom for you. When she is in Domino's she asks for your conizzas!!!'

Well little girl, welcome to the adult world. Logic doesn't always work here.

5. THE CONUNDRUM

Last night I offered a six-year old kid crayons to play with till his pizza arrived. He smugly told me that he was grown up now and doesn't play with crayons. Then a college student came and requested if she could have the crayons. She said she would like to have them till the pizza arrived. Must admit it's a fucked up world!

6. AN ODE TO THE DEAR DEPARTED

This young lady brought her grandmother to the pizzeria. The old lady was diabetic. She had multiple allergies and was a high blood pressure patient. But she insisted on eating all kinds of food. 'I am not going to live long. Let me eat what I want to.' She kept saying. We carefully planned her menu. She wanted to try mint mojito. The young lady was worried. Suddenly I asked her if she would like to have tea with me. The old lady said that she couldn't find it in the menu. I winked and said we keep it for special people. While paying she wanted to pay for the tea as well. I told her it was on me.

After a week the young lady came and informed me sadly that her grandmother had died. Her last meal was the one she had in Pizza-Corner. While dying she remembered me and asked her granddaughter to thank me for the tea. It was a poignant moment. I pointed to the star that was twinkling the most and said, 'That must be your grandma.'

She smiled and squeezed my hand, her eyes moist, she said, 'Thank You.'

✦ ✦ ✦